He caught sight of her in the chair with the baby.

Leaning forward, Garrett peeked over Abby's shoulder at the sleeping baby.

"Do you want to hold her?" she asked.

Garrett's smile vanished, replaced by a wary look that she instantly knew represented a feeling that Garrett Cole wasn't very comfortable with.

"Come on, no turning back now."

She switched Charlotte to a cradling position and stood, placing the tiny bundle in Garrett's arms. His expression gentled as he watched Charlotte sleep, and Abby's heart gave a painful thump. She stepped back, away from him. "No."

"Pardon?" He looked up, his eyes crinkling as his smile returned.

"Nothing." She let out a shaky laugh and picked up her bag. "I've got to go."

These couple of hours with Garrett had been fun. He was smart and compassionate and...nothing.

She was here to heal. To get a family preservation program off the ground.

Not to try to date her best friend's partner— no matter how adorably befuddled he was.

Award-winning author **Stephanie Dees** lives in small-town Alabama with her pastor husband and two youngest children. A Southern girl through and through, she loves sweet tea, SEC football, corn on the cob and air-conditioning. For further information, please visit her website at stephaniedees.com.

Books by Stephanie Dees

Love Inspired

Triple Creek Cowboys

The Cowboy's Twin Surprise
The Cowboy's Unexpected Baby

Family Blessings

The Dad Next Door
A Baby for the Doctor
Their Secret Baby Bond
The Marriage Bargain

Visit the Author Profile page at Harlequin.com for more titles.

The Cowboy's Unexpected Baby

Stephanie Dees

LOVE INSPIRED
INSPIRATIONAL ROMANCE

LOVE INSPIRED®

INSPIRATIONAL ROMANCE

Recycling programs for this product may not exist in your area.

ISBN-13: 978-1-335-48803-9

The Cowboy's Unexpected Baby

Copyright © 2020 by Stephanie Newton

This edition published by arrangement with Harlequin Books S.A.

For questions and comments about the quality of this book, please contact us at CustomerService@Harlequin.com.

Love Inspired
22 Adelaide St. West, 40th Floor
Toronto, Ontario M5H 4E3, Canada
www.Harlequin.com

Printed in U.S.A.

Have not I commanded thee?
Be strong and of a good courage; be not afraid,
neither be thou dismayed: for the Lord thy God
is with thee whithersoever thou goest.
—*Joshua* 1:9

For all the mamas and daddies who open their hearts and homes to unexpected babies, who freely offer their love while expecting nothing in return and who know down to their soul that every child deserves a family.

Chapter One

Garrett Cole stumbled into the kitchen where he'd set the coffee to brew exactly seven minutes before his alarm went off. The last of the water sputtered through the filter as he pulled the coffeepot out and reached for a mug that wasn't there.

He heard a mewling sound and froze. It sounded like a cat. Or a kitten. He thought about investigating, but no—coffee first, then strange sounds. Opening the cabinet, he pulled out a mug and, still half-asleep, went through the coffee ritual. One spoonful of sugar, a splash of vanilla almond milk, stir. Drink. *Yes.*

As the first jolt of caffeine hit his system, he started running the day's schedule in his mind. Juvenile court at ten o'clock. Mrs. Bledsoe at three o'clock to finalize her latest will. The new social worker Wynn hired was dropping by today or tomor—he stopped, tilted his head and listened.

Was it a cat?

At least one single cat would be easier to deal with than the dog who'd had nine puppies under his porch a few months ago. Puppies everywhere. Puppies galore. He and his brothers and new sister-in-law had chased those little rascals all over the ranch and called in every last favor they were owed to find those pups a home.

He took another swig of coffee and listened. Silence.

In Garrett's mind, he had three things going for him: his passion for his work, his dedication to family and his willingness to risk everything for a lost cause. And, boy, did those lost causes find him. Puppies under the house. Parents on their last chance to prove their sobriety. And now, apparently, kittens.

Garrett pulled open the door and stepped outside, stopping short when he heard the small cry again.

He spun slowly to the left.

It wasn't a cat.

Garrett blinked, his mind refusing to process what he saw. There was an actual *baby* on his front porch. He took a step closer and closed his eyes. It had been a rough week—lots of late hours prepping for the last court case. Maybe he wasn't as awake as he thought he was. But when he opened his eyes, it was still there— a very tiny baby in a pink outfit, rocking gently on the porch swing in its car seat.

He spun around, peering into the woods, sure his brothers were about to jump out laughing at how good they'd gotten him. But he saw nothing, heard nothing— only the sound of the wind rustling through the dried stalks of the cornfield yet to be cut and the rooster crowing in the distance.

In the car seat, the baby was starting to squirm.

Garrett stabbed his fingers through hair that was forever in need of a cut, the same two questions on repeat in his mind. Who left a baby on his porch? And what was he supposed to do with her?

The tiny face was getting redder, the grunts and whimpers coming more often. Garrett had almost no experience with babies, but he was pretty sure that wasn't a good sign.

Picking up the seat and the diaper bag sitting next to it, he carried her—pink clothes, so it had to be a girl, right?—into the house. By the time he set her down again on the coffee table, the fussing had turned to full-out wailing, her color going from red to blotchy purple.

Garrett stared at her for a second, indecision paralyzing him. He had no idea what to do. Fingers shaking, he opened the diaper bag and tried to remember what he knew about babies, the sum total of knowledge coming from the few hours he'd spent with his brother Devin's four-month-old twins.

"If they're crying, there are three reasons," Devin had said, ticking them off on his fingers. "Diaper. Dairy. Daddy."

Garrett had rolled his eyes at his brother's alliterative description. Now he wished he'd paid more attention. What did that even mean? He grabbed his phone from the coffee table and shot a text to Devin. Need you. Now.

Okay, three *D*s. Diaper, that one was easy. The baby could be wet or need a change. And yes, there were diapers in the bag!

But dairy? He chewed his lip as he dug through the bag. That had to be milk.

"Oh, you're hungry!" He grinned at her like he'd made a breakthrough scientific discovery. She was unimpressed, the crying ratcheting up to a decibel he had no idea a child could reach.

Frantic now, he went back to the bag, searching the pockets in desperation. *Nothing.* He looked inside. There were a couple of little outfits, but he didn't see a bottle. With a frustrated grumble, he picked up the bag and shook the contents onto the couch cushion.

Finally, he found two small prefilled bottles, the kind Devin's twins had when they first left the hospital. He picked up another small package with the nipple, screwed it on to the top of the bottle and set it on the coffee table.

He unlatched the buckles, freed her arms from the straps of the car seat and gingerly lifted her out. One hand under her backside and the other behind her head, he held her like a bomb that could explode any second. Come to think of it, he was pretty sure he'd be less freaked out holding a bomb than he was holding this screaming baby. A baby he'd just found on his front porch.

Going on pure instinct and vague memory, he moved her into the crook of his elbow and picked up the bottle. As soon as he touched her mouth with the nipple, she latched on and began to drink, her distraught cries subsiding except for a few lingering shuddery breaths.

She looked up at him with bottomless blue eyes, tears still pooling in the corners.

"I'm sorry," he whispered. He eased into a chair and stared, shell-shocked, at the wall across from him.

Whose baby was this? He ran through his list of clients in his mind. Would one of them be so desperate that they would leave a baby on his doorstep?

His head jerked up as the front door swung open.

"I need coffee. What's so important that…" His brother Devin limped into the room, his voice trailing off as he spotted the bundle in Garrett's arms. "Uh, that's a baby."

"Brilliant deduction."

Devin shot him a look and continued to the kitchen. He took a mug out of the cabinet and filled it with coffee before he came back to the living room and sat down in the chair across from Garrett. "Yours?"

"What? No! I walked outside and she was there, on the porch." His voice sounded panicky, even to his own ears, but that was probably because he *was* panicking.

"Why's all that stuff on the couch?"

"She was screaming and I couldn't find the bottles so I dumped everything out."

"I get it, trust me. But it looks like you've got it under control now." Devin reached over and picked a white envelope up from the floor. "What's this? Want me to open it?"

"Yeah, go ahead." The baby sucked the last little bit of milk from the bottle. Her eyes were closed now, her little body finally relaxed. "Wait. She finished the bottle. Am I supposed to burp her now?"

"Just put her on your shoulder and pat her back." Devin didn't look up from the papers. "The baby's name is Charlotte. She's two weeks old. Wow. Two weeks?"

"Who thought it was a good idea to leave a two-week-old baby with me?" Garrett's voice rose in alarm as he patted the back of the tiny little girl.

"Well, there are some legal papers here that look like someone thought it was a good idea to leave a baby with you forever. You're listed as Charlotte's legal guardian."

His brother laughed. "Well…this will put a damper on your merry-go-round of girlfriends."

Garrett scowled.

"You know I haven't been out with anyone si—" His mouth dropped open. *"Guardian?"*

His mind would not process this. Finally, he said, "The mother's name?"

"Brooklyn Brady. Do you know her?"

Garrett slumped back in the seat, one hand holding the baby in place on his chest. "I know her. I was her law guardian until she aged out of foster care. I didn't even know she was pregnant."

Garrett's eyes stung. Brooklyn had been his client for as long as he'd been doing family law. She'd grown up in foster care with her own mother dropping in and out just often enough to keep the courts from terminating parental rights. Brooklyn had finally been freed for adoption, but by that time she was an angry fifteen-year-old and no one wanted to adopt her.

"There's a letter here for you." Devin looked up from the papers in his hand. "How old is this girl?"

"Eighteen." Garrett's emotions had been on a roller coaster—no, roller coaster wasn't descriptive enough. This morning had been more like one of those slingshot rides that shot you into the sky and bounced you around on rubber bands until you got sick.

Mostly now, he just felt sad. Sick, but sad.

"She says she can't give Charlotte a stable life. She can't give herself one. So she's leaving Charlotte with you because…" His brother cleared his throat. "…because you're the only person who ever made her feel like she wasn't damaged goods. Like she was worth caring about. That's why she left the baby with you."

Garrett had tried to do his best for Brooklyn, but he felt like he'd failed her. She'd aged out without a family, without anyone to guide her and be her support system. She'd kept in touch with him for a while but when she'd stopped calling, he hadn't tried very hard to find out why.

"What are you going to do?"

Garrett *wanted* to settle down. He wanted to know that when he came home from work, someone would be there waiting for him. He hadn't found the right person yet—not for lack of trying—a fact his brothers teased him about incessantly. But he was tired of being alone.

He wanted a family. He just hadn't expected it to happen like this. "If the paperwork holds up?"

"Yeah."

Garrett tucked a sleeping Charlotte into the crook of his arm. She barely stretched from his elbow to his wrist. So tiny and so dependent. He blew out a shaky breath and looked up at his brother. "Guess I'll have to learn how to change a diaper."

Abby Scott strolled down the main street of Red Hill Springs, Alabama, getting her first look at the little town where she'd taken a temporary grant-funded job as the town social worker. Her golden retriever Elvis walked calmly beside her. He was on a leash, but didn't need to be. He wouldn't budge from her side unless she asked him to.

Together, she and Elvis had traveled almost constantly for the last eight years, providing animal-assisted therapy in disaster areas. She was the expert in mental health, but Elvis was her partner, the one who really made the kids she worked with feel better.

Compared to the places she usually stayed, the small house she'd rented in Red Hill Springs had seemed positively luxurious when she'd stopped by this morning to drop off her stuff.

The town was charming with the carefully curated storefronts and restaurants. There was even a pediatrician's office on this street. For a moment, she wondered if he saw a lot of childhood trauma in his practice and then shoved that thought right out of her head. She'd find out soon enough.

The call from Mayor Wynn Grant asking her to set up a program in their town to make sure no kids slipped through the cracks had come at a perfect time. She was on leave from her job at the disaster relief organization, making her own mental health a priority for a few months.

Her last assignment had been hard. She needed a reset. Brain. Heart. Body. Faith.

A car door closed behind her and she turned around to see her old friend Wynn, hair flying, heels clacking, arms stretched out to sweep her into a whirling hug.

Abby stepped back, laughing. "You haven't changed a bit since our days on Capitol Hill, Mayor Grant."

"Ha! I've seen the bags under my eyes in the mirror. I know that's not true." Wynn locked arms with Abby and drew her down the street. "Come on. My office— *your* new office—is just a few doors down. You might need to pick up a few things before you start next week."

"I can't wait to see it. You're happy? You look happy."

Wynn smiled as she pushed open a door next to a small brass sign that said Cole & Grant, and underneath, in smaller letters, Attorneys at Law. "I am. I'll tell you all about it. But we have plenty of time to talk while you're here. I'm so excited!"

Abby really didn't have to ask. She could see the happiness and peace radiating from her friend's face. A knot formed in Abby's stomach, the same knot she'd been pushing down, pushing away, for months. She hadn't felt at peace in a long time and a part of her was afraid she would never find it again. She'd seen so much, experienced so much. Her hand inadvertently went to her side, where the scar from the bullet wound that had been her ticket home still ached.

Her job as a social worker on a disaster relief team wasn't made up of predictable pieces. It was random and exhausting, but also meaningful. Her decision to go on a training mission to a refugee camp near the Syrian border had seemed like more of the same. She'd never worried much about her own safety. Danger to herself had always seemed sort of abstract.

Until it wasn't.

Wynn's voice dragged her back to the present. "So this is it. Nothing extravagant. But we have Bess—the best executive assistant in the southeast. Bess, this is my friend Abby. She's joining our staff here for a few months—unless we can convince her to stay."

"Nice to meet you." Bess was young and pretty, and from the looks of her spotless desk, frighteningly efficient. She picked her bag up from a hook on the back of the chair. "Wynn, I have a dentist appointment this morning, but I'll be back as soon as possible."

"Garrett should be in any minute. We've got it covered." Wynn turned to Abby. "I have a few minutes for coffee, if you do, Abs."

"Of course." Abby followed Wynn to the coffeepot against the back wall and leaned against the counter while her friend filled two mugs. "I love this. I love all of it. The town, the office, your happy face. I'm so glad I'll get to be here for a few months to enjoy it."

"Me, too." Wynn handed her a cup of coffee with a speculative look Abby recognized. "So tell me why you really had six months to give me for this project. I'm thrilled, believe me. But I thought you were planning to go back to your job when your doctor gave you the all clear."

"I was." Abby hesitated. She wanted to go back to work. She found it fulfilling in a way that nothing else in her life ever had been. But being wounded in Syria had changed things, left her feeling helpless in a way she never wanted to feel again. She needed time.

She took a deep breath, about to say just that, as the front door slammed open.

A man struggled through the opening with an infant car seat over one arm. On the other, he'd strung a diaper bag and a half-dozen plastic bags from a discount store.

He was dressed in a suit, but he'd missed a couple buttons on his shirt, which was only tucked in on one side. She narrowed her eyes, glancing over at Wynn. "Client?"

Wynn's eyebrows shot up. "Ah...no. My partner, Garrett. Who doesn't have any kids and is usually fully dressed when he comes to work."

Abby watched as Garrett strong-armed his load onto

a conference table. His dark hair was in haphazard disarray. Behind dark-rimmed glasses, his deep brown eyes were expressive and desperate.

"Garrett, what in the world?" Wynn reached him in time to help him untangle himself from the line of plastic bags. A pink plastic baby bottle tumbled out of the bag and bounced off the concrete floor.

Abby crossed to the table and picked up the bottle, holding it out to Wynn's partner.

He took it from her hand and then looked up, shoulders squaring as he realized he didn't know her. His gaze shot to Wynn, who grinned.

"Garrett, my best friend Abby, our new town social worker. Abby, this is Garrett. And I have no idea who this baby belongs to."

"That would be me. For now. Apparently." Garrett shoved his fingers through longish dark hair, making it stand on end. "I'm her guardian."

"I'm sure there's a story there and I definitely want to hear it," Wynn said. "But right now, I have a date with Judge Morrison."

"You're in court this morning? I was hoping you could watch Charlotte. I have court, too. I'd ask for a continuance, but it's a permanency hearing."

Wynn shrugged into her suit jacket and picked up her briefcase. "I'm sorry, Garrett. I'm cutting it close as it is."

She wrapped her free arm around Abby and cinched her in for a sideways hug. "I'm so glad you're here for a while. It's been too long. I wish I didn't have to go."

"Go do your job. We have time to catch up before I start work next week."

As Wynn blew out the door, an uncomfortable silence stretched. Abby shot Garrett an awkward smile.

"I'm usually a little more together than this." Garrett smiled sheepishly, rubbing the stubble on his chin. "I usually shave."

He was obviously in over his head and since she could understand that, Abby gave him an empathetic smile. "It sounds like you've had quite a morning. Most of the time Elvis and I work in places where there's no running water, so there's a decent chance I wouldn't have noticed anyway."

He looked around the office. "Bess?"

"At the dentist."

His head dropped. He muttered, "Family emergency justifies a continuance and this is most definitely a family emergency."

Was he talking to her?

A second later, he dug his cell phone out of his pocket and snapped off a text. He didn't look up again until he'd shoved the phone back into place in his pocket. His eyes widened when he saw her, like he'd forgotten she was there.

He rubbed his forehead. "Sorry. This morning really threw me. I have no idea what I'm doing."

Abby told herself this wasn't her problem. She told herself not to get involved. She even told herself to think about that long nap she'd promised herself this afternoon. "I could stay. I guess?"

His eyes snapped to hers. "Are you sure?"

The hope in his brown eyes made her glad she'd made the impulsive offer. "Sure. I like babies."

"Do you know how to change a diaper?" His grin

was lightning fast as he turned to unbuckle the baby from the car seat. "Oh, no, I left the diapers in the car."

Abby let out a stunned laugh as he handed her the baby and sprinted out the door. She touched the baby's dimpled chin with one tentative finger. "Hey, little girl."

The baby blinked up at her, a fleeting smile crossing the small face. Just like that, Abby was charmed.

She glanced down at her golden retriever, who waited patiently beside her. His blond eyebrows seemed a little skeptical, even as his tail thumped on the floor. "Oh, come on, she's cute, but we're just helping out for a little while." His expression didn't change. "I mean it. We're not getting sucked into anything, I promise."

Chapter Two

A few minutes later, Garrett kicked open the front door of the office and dragged in the box with the porta-crib. Under his other arm was a box of diapers. "Got 'em."

"Wow. You bought a crib."

"Yeah, I didn't have time to do research this morning. I just bought everything. Too much?"

"I've been out of the country for a while. I think I've forgotten what it's like to have choices and everything available right when you need it." Her voice was soft, her eyes on the baby.

Garrett snuck a glance at her. Short dark brown hair prone to wave, long black eyelashes, pretty hazel eyes that looked just a bit wary. He flipped through the information in his mind that Wynn had shared with him about Abby. Licensed clinical social worker. Disaster relief overseas. Old friends. Wait—she got shot. That's right. She was working in a Syrian refugee camp and somehow got shot.

He gave her a rueful smile. "I'm not usually so impulsive. Or maybe I am, I don't know. Either way, I just remembered you got shot. I'm sorry. That must've been horrible."

Abby made an attempt at a smile. "Yeah, it was pretty bad. I know all the things to do for people who experience traumatic events, but education only goes so far when you're the one with the trauma."

"I was pretty young when my parents were killed in a car accident, but I still remember what it was like to have that safety net pulled out from under me. If you ever want to talk, I'm a good listener."

She nodded but didn't say anything, just looked away.

Okay, then. *Way to go, champ. Batting a thousand.* "So what's next? Maybe I should set up the porta-crib?"

Abby wrinkled her nose. "Actually, I think now might be a good time for Diaper Changing 101."

Gingerly, he leaned forward and sniffed. "Oh, yeah. So what do I do first?"

"I laid out the changing pad and the wipes on the conference table." Abby walked over to the table and, with her hand supporting Charlotte's neck, laid the baby gently onto the mat. "Make sure you hold her head up if you're not cradling her against you."

"Support the neck. Got it." Oh, surely he hadn't been letting Charlotte's head flop around all morning?

Abby stepped to the side and said, "The first thing you do is take off enough clothes so you can change her."

"I think this is a see-one-do-one learning experience. I'll just watch you this time." Garrett mentally crossed his fingers.

"Sure, but you have to take her home with you tonight whether you know how to change a diaper or not."

"You're not nice."

A laugh sputtered out. "Tactfully put. But I get it, it's cool. You'll probably be fine on your own."

"Wait…that came out wrong. You're obviously *very* nice." He shot a grin at Abby and stepped up to the edge of the table. Beads of sweat formed across his forehead as he looked down at the baby, who stared at him with her fist in her mouth. Charlotte's legs were no bigger than his thumb.

"You just have to go for it. She won't break, I promise you."

He could do this, no problem. He'd raised newborn goats and they'd survived. How different could it be? He tucked his fingers under the elastic band at Charlotte's waist, and after a few minutes of wrangling, he managed to get the baby partially undressed. "Now what?"

"Slide the fresh diaper underneath but keep the dirty one under her until…" Abby's voice trailed off as he pulled the soiled diaper out and got the clean one dirty.

"Oh. Oh, no."

She didn't say anything, just handed him another clean diaper. This time, he slid the clean one under and took the wipe she held out.

"Take two. No worries, Charlotte. We got this." He held her feet up, took a swipe and gagged.

Beside him, Abby tried—and failed—to hide the fact that she was laughing at him.

"Hey, feel free to get in here and—" He made another pass at the mess. "Oh, this is awful. She's so wiggly. Stop laughing, Abby."

She held out another wipe. "Here, but be quick about it, or…"

He sighed, and without a word held out his hand for another diaper.

The giggle from Abby started him chuckling and before he knew it, he was laughing, but he got the diaper around the baby and fastened the tabs. When he looked up, he caught a glimpse of Abby's smile and it stopped him in his tracks, made him want to dig deeper and find out what really made her tick.

As if his life wasn't complicated enough.

So that was a big fat no. He was full up on lost causes. He'd tried to help Brooklyn—all that time spent as her law guardian and for what? He was caring for an abandoned baby—*her baby*—and she was nowhere to be found.

He was on lost cause number umpteen thousand forty-two. He didn't have time for any more. Even one with pretty hazel eyes and a sharp sense of humor.

Brushing his fingers across the peach fuzz on Charlotte's head, he picked her up. And the diaper he'd struggled to put on her slid halfway down her legs. "Umm... help?"

"Easy fix." Abby laid the baby back down on the mat and deftly released and refastened the tabs before slipping the leggings back on bird-thin baby legs. "You did great. You just have to make the diaper tighter than you think."

Garrett shook his head. "Not as easy as it looks. How'd you learn to do that?"

"I put myself through college being a nanny." She lifted Charlotte and handed her back to Garrett. "Good to go. You'll be a pro in no time."

He cradled Charlotte in his arms and looked down

at her little face. She was precious, with that dusting of strawberry-blond hair on her head and long blond eyelashes. And that whole ugly diaper business faded from his mind.

His heart squeezed.

Was he really going to be able to do this?

Abby picked up the diaper-changing paraphernalia and tucked it into the diaper bag, trying to ignore the warm feeling in her chest as she watched Garrett's face soften. "So how does one end up being surprise guardian to an infant?"

He glanced up. "She was left on my doorstep this morning."

"What?" Abby gaped at him. It sounded like something from the plot of a TV movie. "Do you know who left her there?"

He swayed back and forth as Charlotte's eyelids fluttered closed. "Her mom is a former client. I was her law guardian when she was in foster care."

"Maybe this is an obvious question, but how'd she know where you live? I'd guess that's not something you share with your clients on a regular basis."

"No. My brothers and I own a ranch and we have some horses and goats and cows. Last spring, we invited a bunch of foster families out for a picnic. Brooklyn was one of those." He shrugged. "It seemed like such a small thing at the time."

"It's a nice thing. I wouldn't second-guess it now." She put her hand on his arm and his dark brown eyes darted up to meet hers. She swallowed hard. "So, um… she just left the baby on your porch?"

"She also left signed papers giving me custody—technically a delegation of parental authority—but I have no idea if that will stand up to scrutiny. To make matters more complicated, I'm a mandatory reporter. I can't just pretend that a baby didn't appear on my front porch. I have to report this to family services."

His eyes were steady behind the lenses of his dark-rimmed glasses and Abby realized that momentary flash of attraction hadn't gone away. Instead, she found herself drawn to find out more about him. His laugh lines told her he was a man who smiled often, his gentleness with the baby revealing a kind heart.

Oh, girl, get a grip on that wild imagination. She had no space in her life right now for any kind of entanglement, romantic or otherwise, even if she did that kind of thing. Which she didn't. She had to focus on rebuilding her life. Or building a new life?

Whatever—she had to focus. "Do you know how to reach the mother?"

"I tried calling her. Or at least the last number I had for her, but I didn't get an answer."

"Tough situation." Abby paused a moment, not sure if she should even ask the next question. "Do you...want to be her legal guardian?"

He looked down into Charlotte's guileless face, raised one shoulder and let it drop with another sigh. "I don't know what I want. I want to make this better—for everyone."

Abby nodded slowly. "I'm familiar with that feeling. If I can help, let me know."

"Thanks." With Charlotte firmly asleep, he laid her

gently into her car seat and eased himself free. "Come on, I'll give you the grand tour."

The office space was open, industrial almost, with three small offices and the receptionist's desk on one side of the room. The walls of the offices were glass panels which, now that she considered it, was a thoughtful choice. Enough privacy for confidentiality but enough visibility for everyone's safety. Something she could appreciate these days.

"Before Wynn joined the practice, the whole space was open. It was just a few chairs and a desk."

By the front door, there was a cozy seating area. Behind that a conference table and, in the very back of the room, a small kitchenette. The overall effect was warmth from the exposed brick and reclaimed wood, but with enough polish that it would give clients a sense they were in good hands. "It's really a remarkable space. I can see that you both had a hand in designing it."

"Thanks. I like it."

A quick look at the baby reassured Abby that Charlotte was still sleeping, so she followed him across the room for a closer look at the individual offices. Elvis lifted his head to track her movement.

"This one is Wynn's, if you couldn't tell from the desk. Her husband Latham made it."

Like Wynn herself, the small office managed to convey chic and approachable at the same time. The desk was a smooth concrete surface over reclaimed wood supports. It was bare except for a closed laptop and a small bird's nest with four hand-carved eggs. "I love it. It looks just like her."

Garrett's office was next to Wynn's. In contrast to Wynn's pristine office, his space was…lived in.

"I like a creative organization system, as you can see." Garrett grinned.

A long wood counter stretched the length of the wall behind his desk. His filing system seemed to be a series of labeled boxes stacked three deep. She snorted a laugh as she noted the huge black cat stretching in the corner, underneath a signed poster of Michael Jordan dunking a basketball.

"Barney Fife came with the place. No idea how old he is, but I'm guessing at least fifteen."

She smiled. "I didn't know you had an office cat."

"Will your dog be okay having a cat around?"

"Elvis likes cats. Worst-case scenario, he just ignores Barney. Best case, they'll be BFFs."

The cat turned one sleepy yellow eye toward her before going back to his nap.

From the door, Garrett said, "He's very demanding."

She laughed again. "I can see that."

"So this one is yours. The desk came out of the historic school. I rescued it before they tore the place down. It's probably at least a hundred years old."

"I like it. It has personality." The two leather chairs were generic but in good shape. She made a mental note to buy a plant and some art for the walls. Maybe a throw rug. Here she had time to make the place—the job—her own. It was a shift in thinking, but a much-needed one. "Oh, there's a dog bed."

"Wynn wanted to make sure that Elvis would feel comfortable here, too. She's really excited about this project. I am too, to be honest. If we can identify ways to help people before they need a lawyer, maybe we can really make a difference in people's lives."

"I agree. I can't wait to get started." Their tour ended back at the conference table. She started picking up the stuff Garrett had bought for the baby earlier this morning. She found two packages of bottles, a can of formula, three different kinds of pacifiers, some baby socks and, even though he wouldn't need it for some time, a baby-proofing kit.

Abby was still staring at the assortment of stuff when a woman carrying a diaper bag and a large translucent plastic tub came in through the front door. Garrett sprang into action and met her at the door, taking the big storage tub out of her hands.

"Thanks, Garrett." The woman's blond hair was piled on top of her head and, despite circles under her eyes, she sent Abby a bright smile. "You must be Abby. I'm Wynn's sister, Jules. It's great to finally meet you."

"Nice to meet my landlord in person." Abby smiled. "I dropped my stuff off at the cottage this morning and came straight into town to meet Wynn. I didn't even have a chance to look around."

"And I got an SOS call from Wynn about Garrett's surprise baby, so I packed up a few things just to get him through." As she spoke, Jules walked to the table and looked into the baby carrier. "Oh, she's precious, Garrett."

Garrett seemed to have things under control now, so Abby picked up her purse. She used a hand motion to call Elvis, who was by her side in an instant. "I guess I need to get going."

He looked up in alarm. "You're leaving? But I haven't learned how to make a bottle yet."

"I think I've got you covered there." Jules unzipped the large diaper bag. "There are some benefits to having a pediatrician for a brother and one of them is free samples. I stopped by his office across the street and filled this bag with little bottles of ready-made formula. They should last a few days, at least."

"Oh, wow, Jules, thank you. I hadn't even thought about the pediatrician. I guess I need to make an appointment for Charlotte."

"You have a lot to learn, but you'll figure it out. We all do, eventually." Jules glanced at the smartwatch on her wrist. "I've got to run, too—I'm due to meet with the restaurant staff—but if you need anything, let me know. Abby, I hope we can get to know each other better while you're here, especially since we're neighbors now."

"Thanks so much, Jules."

With a grin shot back over her shoulder and a quick wave, her new neighbor hustled out the door and down the sidewalk. And as the door swung shut, Abby heard the first whimper from baby Charlotte.

"I think that's my cue."

"Wait." Panic laced Garrett's voice. "Can you get her while I fix the bottle?"

The bottle was easy to prepare thanks to Jules's thoughtful delivery. A quick shake and he was ready to go. He was holding his hands out to take Charlotte to feed her when the phone rang.

"Do you mind giving her the bottle? I'll grab the phone."

Abby hesitated, but took the bottle from his hand and sat down in a chair she toed out from the table. A few seconds later, Charlotte was eating like a champ, her dark blue eyes focused on Abby's face.

After all that Abby had been through, all that she had seen, she would've sworn that her heart was a piece of granite in her chest. She had to be able to stay calm to help the children she counseled, no matter the circumstances.

She'd closed herself off, willed the feelings to go away. And she'd been successful at it until she'd been hit by a bullet. All those walls she'd spent years shoring up had come crashing down, leaving her grieving and exposed. Hyperaware.

Hypersensitive.

Looking into baby Charlotte's tiny, trusting eyes made her want to make promises. But that was one thing she just couldn't do. She'd made a promise to a child once and she would never get over the guilt of not being able to keep it.

Elvis laid his big head on her knee, his deep brown eyes looking into hers as if he knew what she was feeling. He probably did. She was the counselor, but Elvis? He was the magic maker. Even traumatized children relaxed when stroking his silky golden retriever fur. She smiled at him, despite the pain she still grappled with. "I'm okay, don't worry."

Her dog grumbled, turned a few circles and settled, laying his head on her feet. Elvis worked as hard as she did. In fact, it was his willingness to push through his exhaustion and keep working that had convinced Abby she needed to take a break. They *both* needed a rest.

So Abby had written a resignation letter—which her boss had refused to accept, instead sliding it into a desk drawer. She'd then promised she would accept it at the end of six months if Abby was still absolutely certain she wanted to quit. Abby had gone from one natural disaster to another for years, never knowing where she would be from one month to the next. So why did six months seem like such a long time to wait for closure?

Looking back at the baby, Abby realized that Charlotte's eyes had closed again, the bottle slipping out of her mouth. Setting it on the table beside her, she lifted Charlotte to her shoulder. This baby was so new that her legs didn't even unfold when Abby picked her up. But as Abby patted her back, she let out a soft burp and melted into Abby's shoulder.

Abby sighed, too. It felt good to be able to solve Charlotte's immediate problem with a bottle and a burp. So she took advantage of the sweet baby-holding feeling and let it sink in—the muted hum of the HVAC overhead, Elvis's soft snores and the comforting weight of the baby on her chest.

Her eyes popped open as the sound of the phone hanging up interrupted her almost nap. Garrett grinned as he caught sight of her in the chair with the baby. His long legs ate up the distance across the room.

Leaning forward, he peeked over her shoulder at the sleeping baby. Elvis lifted his head, suspicious of this man getting so close to her, his eyes unerringly following Garrett's movements.

"Do you want to hold her?"

Garrett's smile vanished, replaced by a wary look

that she instantly knew wasn't a feeling that Garrett Cole was very comfortable with.

"Come on, no turning back now."

She switched Charlotte to a cradling position and stood, placing the tiny bundle in Garrett's arms. His expression gentled as he watched Charlotte sleep, and Abby's heart gave a painful thump. She stepped back, away from him. "No."

"Pardon?" He looked up, his eyes crinkling as his smile returned.

"Nothing." She let out a shaky laugh and picked up her bag. "I've got to go."

These couple of hours with Garrett had been fun. He was smart and compassionate and… She was here to heal. To get a family preservation program off the ground.

Not to try to date her best friend's partner—no matter how adorably befuddled he was.

Chapter Three

Three days later, thanks to Abby's expert tutelage, Garrett had the diaper changing down. He could change a diaper like a champ, he thought. It was the rest of his life that was going down the tubes.

This week had been the longest of his life and it was only Thursday afternoon. Rather than go home to his tiny empty cabin, he'd gone to the home where he'd grown up, where his brothers still lived, hoping a visit would take his mind off of all the unknowns.

He stuffed Charlotte's legs back into the leg holes of her sleeper and zipped it. Sliding one hand under her head and the other under her bum, he lifted her up. "Time!"

Devin's head jerked up from where he was snapping the twins into their pajamas. "What? Not possible. You're still an amateur."

Garrett's sister-in-law Lacey looked up from the book she was reading. "I think he has an advantage since he only has one baby, honey."

With a laugh, Garrett plopped Charlotte into one of

the bouncy seats Lacey and Devin had for the twins and turned on the vibrating gizmo. "The zippered outfits that Jules gave me were a game changer."

"Zippers?" Devin narrowed his eyes. "Mine are wearing pants!"

Garrett raised his eyebrows and made a zipping sound as he reached for his mug.

"Don't encourage him, Garrett, because the next thing that happens is he'll be headed into town to get new clothes for Phoebe and Eli so he can beat your time." Lacey closed her book as Phoebe started to fuss, but she paused to drop a kiss on Devin's head. "I'll get the bottles."

"She does know me well." Devin buckled Eli into the other seat, lifted Phoebe to his shoulder and stood, bouncing. "Well, you seem to be taking all this in stride."

Garrett nearly spit his cold coffee out. "Really? Because I feel like I'm slowly sinking in quicksand while the rest of my world is falling apart and struggling is only dragging me in deeper."

"That seems kind of dramatic." Devin took the bottle Lacey handed him and settled on the sofa with Phoebe as Lacey picked Eli up to feed him. "Like what?"

"Like, I need to talk to Charlotte's mom and I can't get her to respond to my texts or calls. Like, just about the time I open a file and really start working, it's time for feeding or diapering or bouncing or she needs her pacifier."

His voice was climbing. "She only sleeps in thirty-minute snatches. I have her seventy-two-hour hearing tomorrow in family court—when the judge will decide if she needs to be in foster care—and the most efficient assistant in history is one more poop explosion away from quitting. And if she quits, Wynn will kill me and I can't let that happen because I have a baby now." He ran out of breath about the time he ran out of words and at the exact time that he realized his brother and Lacey were both staring at him, eyes wide.

He sighed and stabbed his fingers into his hair as he muttered, "Sorry."

"Don't be sorry, Garrett. We're your family. Who else are you going to tell?" Lacey, beside Devin on the sofa, elbowed her husband, who cleared his throat.

"Yeah, babies are hard. What can we do to help?"

Garrett let his head fall back against the leather seat of the recliner. "You guys have your hands full with your own kids. I've seen Lacey making cookies in the middle of the night to sell at the farm stand and I know how slim your margin is. I'll figure it out."

"There's always day care, right? Where does Wynn take A.J.?" Devin asked.

"To Community Church, but they have to be six weeks old to go there. And who knows if I'll have her then, or if they'll even have a space for Charlotte when the time comes."

Lacey lifted a sleeping Eli to her shoulder and stood. "Give yourself some grace, Garrett. Even people who have time to plan are overwhelmed with the reality of what it's like to have a baby."

He nodded, his gaze going to Charlotte asleep in the bouncy seat. She was so little, the size of one of his hands, and just so dependent on him for everything.

Yeah. *Overwhelming* was a good word for it.

His brother Devin said, "I bet one of the church ladies would be willing to babysit."

"Normally, yes, but they're all in Branson, Missouri for ten days. Some kind of quilting conference and then they're hitting a bunch of shows. Their timing is terrible." Garrett heard the words he'd just said and wanted to gobble them back. "That was a joke."

Eli's pacifier popped out and Lacey bent her knees and snagged it before it could hit the floor. "Ooh, I know—what about the new social worker, the one who kept Charlotte a couple of days ago while you were in court? Has she started her job yet?"

"You mean Abby?" A smile started at the corner of his mouth. She'd saved his skin that first day and he'd thought of her often since then. She didn't even know him, but her quick humor and totally unfounded confidence in his ability had made Garrett feel more in control.

"See? Right there. There's the look I was telling you about." Devin pointed at Garrett. "He makes that face every time she comes up in conversation."

Lacey studied Garrett's expression with a squinty eye. "Hmm. I see what you mean. Very curious."

"You guys are hilarious." Garrett started tossing stuff back into Charlotte's diaper bag. "I'm leaving."

Lacey smiled, clearly amused, but her voice was kind. "Garrett, you're always the first one to step in and help when we need it—when anyone needs it. It's all right to ask for help yourself."

He much preferred being the one doing the helping, but maybe Lacey was right. In any case, he didn't have much choice. He was desperate to find a sitter for tomorrow afternoon. "Okay, I'll text her."

Abby's shiny dark hair and pretty hazel eyes came to mind. She was the silver lining to this absurd situation if there was one. And if he had to ask for help, at least he'd get to see her again.

Abby stirred sugar into her coffee, the very act seeming like a luxury. She'd had instant coffee in the refugee camp, and she could almost always find a way to boil some water, but it wasn't the same as freshly brewed. Not even close.

A knock at the door startled her and she glanced at the clock on the oven. Ten thirty! She'd expected it to be seven o'clock. Maybe it was a good thing she was starting work on Monday.

The knock came again. She glanced down at her yoga pants. Old, but the holes were all in discreet locations. Her feet were bare, toenails in the screaming pink neon polish that had been an impulse when Wynn had dragged her to the salon for a much-needed pedicure the day before.

With a quick fluff of her bedhead, she wrapped her fuzzy gray sweater around herself and took a quick peek through the peephole in the door. Garrett stood on her doorstep, his collar turned up against the wind, the handle of the baby carrier gripped in one hand.

She tugged the belt on her sweater a little tighter and pulled the door open just as he was turning away. "Hi."

Garrett turned around, his beaming smile fading just a bit as his eyes traveled from her disheveled hair to her bare toes. "I think maybe… I came at a bad time. I texted you."

"Not a bad time. This is just me, not working, and I turned my phone off because my former boss keeps asking me to come back to work." Tucking a piece of hair behind her ear, she shivered. "I thought winter was supposed to be mild in Alabama. It's freezing out there. Come in, please."

He followed her into the living room and she saw him take note of the dishes in the sink, the pillow and blanket on the couch. Inwardly, she might have cringed a little, but what was the point? "Sorry for the mess. I'm making up for lost sleep. Like four years' worth. So what can I do for you? Or is this a social call?"

Garrett placed the baby carrier on the kitchen table and took a deep breath as he folded back the cover. "Not exactly."

She leaned forward to sneak a peek at Charlotte before she leaned back against the counter and crossed one ankle over the other. "Okay?"

He rubbed one thumb across his lips. "Wow, this is more awkward than I thought it would be. I need help. I've asked all the church ladies and pretty much everyone else I know and I can't find a babysitter for Charlotte. I know it's not fair to ask, but is there any way you could help me out this afternoon?"

"You talk so fast." Abby crossed to the table and unbuckled the car seat straps. She lifted Charlotte into her arms, smiling down at her. "Hi, baby girl."

"Yeah, sorry. Hazard of the job. Judges never give you enough time to say what you need to say." Garrett sat down in one of the chairs at the kitchen table. His cheeks were ruddy with cold, or maybe a little chagrin at having to ask for help.

Abby swayed back and forth as Charlotte's eyelids drooped closed. Garrett was clearly overloaded and Charlotte was just sweetness. "I can watch her. I don't mind."

Garrett closed his eyes for a second and she wondered if he was praying. When he opened them, he said, "You're sure? It's just for the afternoon."

"Truthfully, I've been in a lot of situations where I wished there was something I could do. If this actually helps you, I'm glad to do it."

"The seventy-two-hour dependency hearing for her is at two o'clock."

"That's fine. I don't have anything else to do. And I'm well rested." Abby's lips twitched, but she kept patting Charlotte, not sure the baby was firmly asleep yet. "What happens at the hearing?"

"A social worker from the Department of Human Resources will tell the judge what happened and make a recommendation to the court. I think they'll recommend that she be officially placed with me." He nudged his glasses farther up his nose and stabbed his fingers into his hair in a motion that she realized telegraphed his stress. "Then the judge will make a decision. He could leave Charlotte with me since we have the papers from her mom. Or he could decide that Charlotte would be better off with foster parents. I really have no idea. This situation isn't one I've come across before."

"Do you want to keep her?"

The question echoed the one she'd asked him the first day and again Garrett paused. His eyes lingered on Charlotte's little face and his eyes softened before he nodded. "Yeah. I want to keep her. I may be the strangest choice for a guardian anyone's ever made, but she's safe with me."

"Good. I can see why her mom chose you."

Garrett blinked and then he grinned. When he smiled, it wasn't just his lips. His smile broke through the winter gloom, brightening the whole room. "Thanks, Abby. I appreciate that. I've got to run. I'll be back as soon as I can."

"Just text me when you're done and I'll bring her to your office. I need to get out of the house anyway."

"Perfect. I'll leave the car seat base on the front porch." He took a moment to brush his fingers across Charlotte's forehead and then was gone, leaving her staring at the closed door.

Okay, so he was really attractive. It had been a long time since she'd been around anyone other than fellow disaster relief workers and they had been as exhausted and careworn as she was.

That didn't mean a flirtation was a good idea. In fact, it was a very bad idea. His smile might warm a room, but everyone knew that getting too close to the sun would burn you.

Garrett leaned on the counter where Bess worked, talking into the phone she handed him while he texted on his cell phone. He heard the door open and turned to see Abby coming in the office door. He quickly ended the conversation, hung up the phone and crossed to her, lifting the heavy infant seat from her hand. "Everything go okay?"

Abby grimaced. "I think maybe she's hungry. She cried all the way here."

Little hiccups could still be heard coming from underneath the stretch cover over the car seat. Garrett pulled the cover back to peek inside. "Aw, Charlotte. What's the matter?"

As soon as she heard Garrett's voice, a thin wail rose from the infant car seat.

"She really isn't happy, is she?" Garrett shifted the seat to his elbow and carried her to the conference table. "Are you ready for a bottle?"

When Charlotte responded with increased volume, Garrett laughed and began the process of unbuckling her. "I think that's a yes."

"Thankfully, I made one before I left the house. I had a hunch we might need it."

He lifted Charlotte out of the seat. "Did Miss Abby try to starve you?"

Abby swatted his arm. "Not funny."

Garrett settled into one oversized leather chair in his office, while Abby perched on the arm of the other one, digging the bottle out of the side pocket of the diaper bag.

He gave it a little shake and then let Charlotte have it. She really did eat like she was starving.

"I fed her three hours ago, I promise!" Abby's dark brown hair was pulled back in a low ponytail with little tendrils curling around her face.

She seemed as casually friendly as usual, but that neon pink toenail polish he'd spied this morning seemed to hint that there were facets to Abby's personality he hadn't yet seen. It made him want to poke and dig and figure her out.

Her eyes lingered on Charlotte, the expression on her face thoughtful.

"What are you thinking?"

Her cheeks colored, a dimple at the corner of her mouth appearing and disappearing. "Just that Charlotte's blessed. Not all kids who go through a childhood trauma have someone who cares as much as you do to take care of them."

He wasn't sure how to feel—flattered that she thought he was caring, or concerned that she thought Charlotte could be traumatized. "Do you think I should be worried about Charlotte?"

"Babies recognize their parents from the first moments they're born—their smell, the way their voice sounds. So she's had a loss. But it helps that she has you."

"Is that your professional opinion?" He shifted in the chair, a little uncomfortable with the intensity of her study.

"My experienced opinion. You haven't said… How did things go in court?"

"Okay. Child Protective Services recommended that Charlotte be placed with me, I think partly because of the mother's request. Partly because they know me."

"That's good." Abby frowned. "Right?"

His head bobbed back and forth—not a yes, not a no. "The judge wasn't happy. Technically, Brooklyn abandoned her baby, and while it's understandable that she picked me to leave her with, in a weird way, the judge wants to make sure that she wasn't coerced."

Abby narrowed her eyes. "So, you have to find Brooklyn?"

"Someone does." He tipped the bottle up so Charlotte could drink the last ounce.

"But it seems like she doesn't want to be found."

"Therein lies the problem."

"From a legal standpoint, I guess I can see the judge's point. The situation *is* weird, but…Charlotte's staying with you, right?"

"The judge said CPS could leave her in my care as a kinship provider, but he's given me until the next hearing to come up with proof that Brooklyn made the choice to leave Charlotte voluntarily. And then there's the issue of the dad."

"Who's the dad?"

"Exactly. We have nowhere to start." Garrett made a face. "So that has to be addressed at the adjudicatory hearing as well."

"Which is when?"

"Supposed to be within thirty days or the earliest practical date, which in this case happens to be a little over six weeks from now if it doesn't get continued."

"How do you feel about that?"

His eyes were on Charlotte as she slowly took the last little bit from the bottle. How he felt was as complicated as the case. "I feel guilty that I couldn't just leave it alone, that the mandatory reporter thing took that decision out of my hands. I feel relieved that Charlotte won't be dragged into another foster home with someone she doesn't know. And at the same time, I wonder if I'm making the best choice for her because I don't have any clue what to do with a baby."

Abby's lips curved into a soft smile. "You're doing fine, but all of those feelings seem perfectly valid to me. Any thoughts on where Brooklyn might be?"

"Not a clue."

"I'll think about it. There's got to be some way to find her. In the meantime, I'm gonna get going. I've got to run to the grocery store before I head home." She walked toward the door and turned back to hand him the burp cloth. "Oh—you might need this."

As if on cue, Charlotte burped and Garrett smiled. "Good call. Thanks for keeping her today. I owe you dinner."

"You're welcome. See you Monday."

As Abby walked away, Garrett's eyes followed. She was beautiful and complicated and a part of him wanted to figure out what was really under that shell of serenity.

He shook his head, chuckling under his breath. His brothers teased him about his idealistic streak. He fell in love about as often as other guys washed their clothes. Any other time in his life, he wouldn't have hesitated to ask Abby out. Now?

Even if he did lose his mind and consider it, he had no idea if she was even planning to stay in Red Hill Springs. It was a nonstarter.

They were working together. And maybe…friends?

And that was all he could let it be.

Chapter Four

Abby's first few days at work were spent brainstorming with Wynn—what specifics the program would focus on, how she would get referrals, and people she needed to contact once she had all the pieces in place to begin the actual work.

Most referrals would probably come from teachers and police officers, but family court attorneys like Wynn and Garrett could request appointments for their clients. There were resources out there for all kinds of obstacles people faced. The problem was connecting the resources with the people who needed them and that's where she came in.

It had been a while since she'd felt anything but helpless, but somewhere down inside, there was a bubble of hope. Putting a program like this in place was a bold move for a small town, but one that could really impact the lives of the residents. She was excited to get started.

Her experience working in the refugee camp along the border of Jordan had broken her, for lack of a better word. She hadn't realized how broken she was until she'd finally gotten to her apartment in Atlanta. She'd barely recognized her own home.

She'd been exhausted but she couldn't sleep. Too thin, but food hadn't appealed to her. In the middle of the third sleepless night, when she'd been mindlessly scrolling through social media, she'd seen Wynn's message, asking if she knew any social workers who might be interested in a job like this. She'd called the next morning and two hours later, she'd talked to her boss, (tried to) quit her job and packed her suitcase.

It had been the right decision. After a week in Red Hill Springs—sleeping at night, eating at the café—she was starting to feel not quite so fragile, like the pieces of herself were slowly knitting back together.

"Knock, knock." Garrett opened the door to her office. He was holding two white paper bags, which he placed on her desk.

She leaned toward him. "You know that's not actually the same as knocking, right?"

"Yes, but I brought goodies from the Hilltop Café. Doughnut or cupcake?"

"Which one has frosting?"

"Oh, please. Who do you think I am? Both."

She found herself smiling, another sign that she was reentering the land of the living, and a not-uncommon occurrence around Garrett. "In that case, please do come in. I'll have the doughnut."

"Good choice." He handed her the doughnut still in the wrap and pulled out the cupcake, vanilla with white frosting, before dropping into the chair opposite her. Peeling back the paper, he took a gigantic bite.

With her doughnut halfway to her mouth, she stopped to watch.

In two more bites, he'd finished it off and caught her watching him as he licked frosting off his thumb. He laughed, wiped his mouth with the back of his hand and brushed the crumbs off his coat. "Two brothers. I had to learn to be fast when there were treats around. Do you have any siblings?"

"In a way, I do. I have some half siblings that are a lot younger. And I grew up with my cousins. My mom and I lost our house to a tornado when I was five. I lived with my grandma for a while, and then with my aunt and uncle." She took a bite of the doughnut and pointed at it with the other hand. "Mmm, really good."

His eyebrows drew together. "I have so many questions. Were you in the house at the time?"

"Yes. We were in the bathroom under the stairs. It was the only part of the house that survived."

He let out a low whistle. "That's extreme. You didn't go back to live with your mom?"

"No. My mom got married the next year." Elvis nosed her hand and leaned into her leg. She took another bite of the light-as-air doughnut and sighed in appreciation.

"So?"

She put the rest of the doughnut down and brushed the sugar off her hands. "So, nothing. You asked if I had siblings. And the answer is, kind of. We're not that close, though. My life up to this point has been pretty different than most people's."

"You could say that. You gonna eat that?" When

she shook her head, he picked up the other half of her doughnut and scarfed it down. "Where was your dad?"

"He was military. Killed in a training accident when I was just a baby." She realized Elvis was standing beside her and wondered if her voice had betrayed some tension that she hadn't even realized she was feeling. Her dog was sensitive to every nuanced emotion, which was what made him so good at his job.

She sent him back to his bed with a hand signal.

Because she was fine. A lot of kids had chaotic childhoods. It wasn't like she hadn't had food to eat or a roof over her head. Garrett opened his mouth, she could only assume to ask another question, and she didn't want to answer any more questions. "So what's up with you?"

"Oh, right. Why I came to find you. I have a client coming in today. Melanie. I'd love it if you could talk to her while I play with her little boy for a few minutes. She doesn't get a break very often."

She picked up the bakery bag and tossed it into the trash can under her desk. "Sure, I'd love to. What's the story?"

"You know how sometimes the deck is so stacked against you to start with that no matter how much you want to, you can't get ahead?"

Abby looked up. "Yes. Is that what happened to Melanie?"

"Yeah. She's on a safety plan with Child Services. She made some questionable life choices, but she wants to do right by her kids. You're gonna love Nash. He's four and he has cerebral palsy but it hasn't slowed him down much. He's a little carrottop with a pistol-ball personality to match."

"So basically, you want me to find out what needs she still has and connect her with the resources?"

"Exactly." In the other room, Charlotte started to cry. "Oops, that's my cue."

He was gone with as little fanfare as he'd arrived, but she realized she felt good, like she could breathe. And she knew it wasn't just gaining distance from all she'd been through. It was a job where she knew she could make a difference. It was doughnuts and laughter and baby snuggles and…it was Garrett.

For some reason, it was Garrett. In the back of her mind, she heard an alarm bell go off that said this is different, *he* is different. But she wasn't going to listen to it, not right now. Right now, she was going to take Elvis outside for a quick walk and wait for her first client to arrive.

Garrett met Melanie at the door as she tried to maneuver a very small wheelchair. Nash was bouncing in the seat.

"Garrett!"

"Hey, buddy." He held out a fist and Nash smashed it.

"He's been so excited to get to come to your office." Nash's mom looked like a teenager with her hair pulled back in a ponytail.

"Glad you could make it." He'd been her court-appointed attorney for the past year and she was doing good. Trying. But trying didn't mean succeeding. He was here to make sure she had everything she needed to succeed.

Abby opened the door to her office and she and Elvis

started toward them. The golden retriever's tail was wagging a mile a minute.

Nash's face lit up as he saw the dog. "Doggie. Mama, doggie!"

"I see, Nash. He's a pretty doggie." To Garrett, she said, "He's been begging for a dog, so his day is made."

"This is Elvis. He loves to play with boys." Abby gave Elvis a hand signal. As he laid his head in Nash's lap, the little boy squealed with excitement. To Melanie, she said, "Hi, I'm Abby. I work with Garrett."

"Melanie. And this is Nash. He's a little excited to meet your dog."

"Elvis loves to meet new people, so I think he's pretty excited, too."

Garrett leaned over and stage-whispered, "Nash, Elvis is so soft, you could use him as a blanket!"

Nash squinted up at Garrett, clearly thinking that through before he giggled. "Uh-uh. Doggies can't be blankets!"

Abby shook her head at Garrett, but she had a twinkle in her eye, so he'd count that as a win on two fronts. He clasped his hands together. "I have a surprise for you guys."

He'd worked for weeks trying to scrape together funding for a specially made stroller for Nash, one that would accommodate his baby sister as well. He brought it out of his office into the open space near the conference table.

Melanie's eyes widened. "Garrett, what is that?"

"Hopefully, the solution to your problems."

"Seriously?" Her eyes filled with tears and she put a hand out. "Garrett, you know I can't pay for this."

"Don't worry about that. Let's see how it works." In one quick motion, Garrett popped open the stroller and locked the seat into place.

The sound caught Nash's attention and he looked up. "What's that?"

"A new stroller. Try turning it around, Melanie."

She turned it with one hand and looked up in wonder. "Oh, it just glides."

Garrett grinned as he reached for a couple of levers near the back wheels and folded a smaller seat into place. He had a new appreciation these days for baby products that were so idiotproof even he could work them. "And this is the sibling seat. Little sister gets to sit here."

Melanie's face crumpled, her eyes filling with tears.

"Melanie?" Garrett's smile faded.

"I don't know how you did this…" She sniffed, visibly struggling for control. "It will change everything. No more missed appointments."

"Wanna ride. Garrett, I wanna ride." Nash untangled his fingers from Elvis's fur and held his arms up.

Melanie laughed. "Hang on, little man. I got you."

After Nash was unbuckled, Garrett reached down and lifted Nash, placing him in the seat.

"Awesome!" The little boy let out a delighted laugh. "Go, Garrett. Ride."

Garrett looked at Abby. "I could take him for a quick spin around the block, to try it out."

"I think that might be necessary." She laughed as Nash bounced up and down in the seat. Garrett caught him as he launched himself into midair.

"Dude. You have to sit still while I buckle you!"

While his fingers were busy with the buckles, Garrett looked up at Melanie. "Abby's the new social worker in our office. If it's okay with you, I asked Abby if she had time to talk to you this morning."

The smile on the young mom's face faded. "Sure, I guess."

Abby put her hand on Melanie's arm. "Don't worry. It's just a casual visit. Would you like a cup of coffee?"

"Sure, thanks." She followed Abby to the kitchenette but looked back toward the door where her little boy was rocking back and forth in the new stroller.

"We won't be long." Garrett double-checked the buckles holding Nash into the seat. "No more trying to pretend you're an astronaut, hear me?"

Nash giggled. "Three, two, one..."

"Blast off!" Garrett blew through the front door, pulling it closed behind him as they raced down the sidewalk. The ecstatic laugh from the four-year-old in the seat told him he'd definitely made the right decision on the stroller.

He gave a quick glance back at the office. He knew Abby was a pro and together she and Elvis were a formidable team, but it was his first time trusting one of his clients with her. Melanie's confidence was still a little shaky. He hoped he was doing the right thing.

Abby handed Melanie a mug of coffee. "Sit down with me? I bet you don't have much time to rest with Nash around, not to mention your little girl. How old is she?"

"Nova's almost six months old. She's with a neighbor right now." Melanie followed Abby into her office, pausing to look at the pictures Abby had hung on the wall the day before.

Abby sat in one of the chairs that she'd moved into a conversational grouping. Elvis sat beside her, his attention glued to her face. "Those are photos of people I've met at some of the disaster areas I've worked in over the years."

"I can see the destruction in the background, but they look so… I don't know, strong?"

"Some of the people in those photos lost everything, but despite that, they were still standing. It's a powerful statement."

"I can so relate to that." Melanie sat in the chair next to Abby, the wariness gone from her face. She was young, early twenties maybe, but the way she carried herself made her seem much older.

With a barely perceptible motion of her hand, Abby released Elvis to go to work. He sat in front of the young mom and tilted his head. Melanie smiled at him. "Hi, buddy."

He nosed her hand and when Melanie reached out to scratch him, Abby knew the connection had been made.

A smile played across Melanie's face as she rubbed one of Elvis's ears. She kept her eyes down, but she said, "I don't know what Garrett told you…"

"He didn't tell me much. Truly."

"I'm on a safety plan with the social services people, and Garrett's my attorney. When we went to court, he fought for me to get to keep my kids with a caseworker checking in on us every month."

"I don't want to be nosy, but if you want to talk about it, I'm a good listener."

The young mom blew her thin bangs out of her eyes and shook her head as if she wanted to negate the memory itself. "My fiancé got high with his friends and came to the hospital when Nova was born. He got a night in jail and I got a caseworker. I had to choose between keeping my children or keeping him. Getting rid of him was the easiest choice I ever had to make."

Melanie had one hand deep in Elvis's fur now, the other one smoothing the small hairs on his forehead. "What was hard was that our car was in my fiancé's name. Without a car, I missed some of Nova's well-baby checkups and that brought the caseworker back to my house."

"Oh, wow. That must be so scary."

"It is—was. The safety plan says I have to take the kids to the doctor and to their therapy appointments on time. The caseworker comes to visit. And we have to go back to court in six months."

"And where does the stroller fit in?"

There was silence for a moment, the struggle to rein in her emotions once again visible on Melanie's face. Finally, she looked up with a small shrug. "I couldn't get on the bus with both kids because I couldn't push Nash's wheelchair and a stroller at the same time. And I couldn't lift the wheelchair if I had Nova in a carrier. I just—I couldn't do it. Someone at church let me borrow a double stroller, but Nash needs more support than a normal stroller can give him."

"What a rough time for all of you. Anyone would be reeling after all that."

"You think so?" Melanie's shoulders slumped, but hope flared in her eyes. "Do you know how much that stroller was? Ten thousand dollars. I could never have bought that for him. And I guess I just worry how I can be a good mom if I can't provide what my kids need."

"Melanie," Abby said gently, "your kids need you, not what you can buy for them."

Melanie's sigh turned into a sob. Elvis nuzzled her chin with his nose, eliciting a strangled laugh.

A squeal of joy reached them from just outside the office. Melanie immediately straightened, swiped tears from her face and smoothed her shirt into place. "I don't want Nash to think I'm worried."

As the boys came in the front door, Abby held out a business card to Melanie. "Write down everything you need to really feel like you have a handle on life. Then call and make another appointment with me. There are resources out there and my job is to connect you with them."

Hope flared in the young mom's eyes. "You're serious?"

"One hundred percent." She paused, looked back at the photos on the wall. "The people in those photos? You're strong, just like they are. Things have happened that you need to take care of, but you're still standing."

Nash shouted from the front door. "Mama! Come see!"

Melanie tucked Abby's card into her back pocket, swallowing hard before looking up. "Thank you."

Abby heard her laughing at the engine sounds Nash made as she walked back to meet him. She hoped Melanie would take her up on the offer. Their family, who because of circumstances mostly beyond their control needed help to get back on their feet, was exactly the kind Abby had been brought in to help.

As Garrett walked Nash and Melanie to the door, Abby heard Charlotte waking up in the porta-crib in Garrett's office and went to check on her. The baby girl had a decidedly crabby look on her face.

"Hi, Charlotte. I bet you need a clean diaper after such a long nap, don't you?" She reached into the crib and picked Charlotte up. The change was easy with Garrett's office nursery setup, but clearly, a dry diaper was not what Charlotte wanted. Her cries were getting progressively louder and more annoyed.

Abby picked her up again and tried the pacifier. Charlotte sucked it for a few seconds before spitting it out. "Oh, baby girl, you are mad, aren't you?"

From the door, Garrett held out a bottle. "She's probably ready for this."

"I'd say so." She took it from Garrett and offered it to the hungry baby.

Over the bottle, Charlotte scowled as if she couldn't possibly understand what took Abby so long to get it right. Abby laughed. "Hey, I'm not the one in charge of the bottles."

"She's opinionated." Garrett dropped into the chair behind his desk. "Wow. Nash wore me out. Did you and Melanie have a good conversation?"

"I think so. Elvis is kind of a genius at getting people to talk." She studied Garrett's face, so handsome with that quick smile that went all the way to his eyes.

"I'm sure it's all Elvis."

"Melanie's doing her best to take care of her kids.

That's gonna be a lot easier with that fancy stroller you got her. How'd you pull that off?"

"It's just a stroller." He picked a file up from his desk and spun around to put it away.

"A ten-thousand-dollar stroller?"

He glanced back at her. "Where did you get that idea?"

"Melanie."

"Oh." He shrugged. "It wasn't a big deal. I called in some favors. Asked for some donations. Got a small grant. It was a little legwork, but the end result is that Melanie can get her kids where they need to go."

"A car would've been cheaper."

"Yeah, but then it would've been for Melanie and she probably wouldn't have accepted it. A gift for Nash and Nova is a little harder to turn down."

"Smart *and* thoughtful."

"It's all part of the service. Plus, you're gonna get her the rest of the way. We make a great team." He shot her a nonchalant grin.

He wasn't fooling her, though. There was nothing nonchalant about him. He was a full-out idealist and she could feel herself getting sucked into his life, bit by bit. How could she not? He genuinely cared about people and wanted to help. If anyone could understand that, she could.

Garrett was a great guy. A sweet guy. She liked him, but she had to be careful. Because if she wasn't, he would pull her into his windmill-tilting plans and she'd been down that path. Had the bullet wound to prove it.

And that was the last thing she needed right now.

Chapter Five

Garrett got out of his SUV at the ranch, where he was supposed to be meeting his brothers for a look at the current finances. After a scare the year before, when the ranch almost got foreclosed on by the bank, the brothers had solidified their pact that they were in this together. Brotherly competition and ribbing aside, nothing happened on this ranch that didn't get run by all three of them first.

He popped the baby carrier out of its base. Charlotte was out like a light. Frantic bleats sounded from the goat pasture. His first goats, Thelma and Louise, had been joined by siblings and they had a good little crew going. He loved those ornery little rabble-rousers. The first two had been a gift from a client, but the other four he'd adopted just because he got a kick out of them. He scratched Mason's head and pushed Dixon back with a laugh when the persistent goat tried to get into Garrett's pants pockets. "Sorry, guys, no treats today."

And when all of them turned away, he shook his

head. "I know you only love me for food, but you could at least pretend."

Brushing his hand off on his pant leg, Garrett crossed the drive, taking the porch steps two at a time. By the number of cars in the yard, he was pretty sure he'd stumbled unwittingly into Lacey's Bible study night. In fact, he thought he'd spotted Abby's car in the mix. He paused to glance back. And Wynn's?

The door flew open. Devin stood in the doorway, with a baby on one hip, the other strapped to his chest and his cane in the other hand. "Well, are you coming in or not?"

"Wow, I think someone missed their afternoon nap and it wasn't the babies." Garrett strolled into the house, slowly stumbling to a halt as he realized the entire place was decorated in a sickening shade of pink. Balloons, streamers… His eyes lingered on a lace-edged banner hanging above the kitchen door. Slowly, he turned back to face his brother. "Surprise?"

With that, people came pouring out of the farm office, the kitchen and the hall, yelling, "Surprise!"

He staggered backward, his right hand grabbing his heart. Abruptly woken from her nap, Charlotte let out a wail. With an apologetic smile, Abby reached for the carrier. "I'll take her."

His sister-in-law Lacey appeared in the kitchen door with a big plate of pink frosted cookies, followed by Jules Quinn carrying a tower of pastel confections.

"I think I'm starting to sense there's a theme to this gathering." Garrett laughed, shaking his head.

"It's a baby shower." A big laundry basket full of gifts wrapped in pink and white landed in the center of the living room, dumped there by his older brother Tanner.

"I gathered." When Garrett looked up, he caught a glimpse of Abby standing against the wall, about as far as she could get from the hullabaloo and still be in the room, calmly unbuckling his screaming baby from the car seat. Bless her. She wasn't used to this bunch of rowdies. She looked so pretty, an island of calm in this sea of chaos. He took a step toward her.

Wynn appeared in front of him, holding a shiny pink metallic crown with giant faux jewels glued to the points.

"Whoa." He put up a hand to stop her. "I will never get the glitter out of my hair if you put that thing on me."

His partner shrugged, unconcerned. "Suck it up, cowboy. Penny made it for you. You have to wear it."

He searched out Wynn's eight-year-old daughter Penny. "You made this crown for me?"

The little girl's eyes shone, her blond curls bobbing as she nodded her head.

"It's quite lovely," Garrett said, in a British accent, which elicited giggles from his buddy. And since he had no choice, he bent down to let Wynn attach the atrocious thing to his head.

Someone pushed him into the big chair and someone else tossed a gift in his lap. A pink plastic cup filled with some kind of frothy liquid appeared on the table beside him. He sought out Abby again, his eyes meeting hers. He mouthed, "Help?"

A wail went up from one of the many babies in the room. Instantly, attention was diverted from Garrett as all the parents searched out their kids.

"Mine! No worries—happens all the time." Wynn scooped up her toddler, who'd somehow gotten caught underneath the coffee table. She slid into a seat and motioned for Abby to join her, waving a hand at the chair between her and Garrett.

He was pretty sure that the last place Abby wanted to be was at this raucous excuse for a baby shower, much less this close to the center. She gamely joined the group, though, laughing as one of his brothers shouted from across the room, "Just open the presents already."

"Okay, okay," he grumbled. "Nothing like a little destressing with a surprise baby shower for your surprise baby after a long day of lawyering."

He wasn't sure but he thought he heard a little snort from Abby.

Ripping into the first package—from Devin—Garrett pulled out a hot pink T-shirt. He read the slogan out loud. "Tea Parties and Tiaras."

He laughed and a shower of glitter landed on his face and shoulders. "Well, Dev, I've got this crown and I think I have a stash of Earl Grey somewhere in my house, so if anyone wants to join in, it's BYOT. Bring your own tiara."

"All that pink glitter is definitely you," his brother Tanner said dryly as he handed over the next package. "This one's from Wynn."

Garrett tore open the box to reveal a necktie covered in pink pacifiers. "Wow! Thanks, partner. The other lawyers are going to be shaking in their boots when they realize I'm man enough to wear this tie."

Beside him, Abby giggled. He glanced over at her, raising an eyebrow. "Did you know about this?"

Her eyes widened, cheeks staining pink. "Nope."

"Why don't I believe that?"

The next gift, from his pal and pediatrician Ash

Sheehan, revealed a set of tools with pink rubber handles. He couldn't help but laugh. "I see how this is going to go."

From Abby, Lacey and Ash's wife Jordan came the basic necessities: pink bottles. Pink pacifiers. Pink blankets and baby onesies.

So. Much. Pink.

Finally, Wynn's husband Latham handed Garrett a card. Inside was a photograph of a beautiful crib. He glanced up. "You made her a crib?"

Latham shrugged. "Least I could do. Everyone pitched in for the materials."

"Also," Ash spoke up. "You shouldn't be surprised if you find a truckload of diapers on your front porch when you get home. My mom told the Ladies' Auxiliary about the baby and they asked what you needed."

"And you said Cubs tickets but they decided on diapers anyway?"

Ash laughed. "Very funny. You need the diapers more. Trust me."

For the next few minutes, he was inundated with questions and well wishes. It was fun and he was touched, but he hadn't slept in over a week and the noise in here was making his head ache. He was desperate to sneak out the front door for a few minutes of silence.

He looked around for Abby to see if she wanted to join him, but she—and Charlotte—were gone.

Abby rocked the porch swing idly with her toes as Charlotte took her bottle. The quiet was a relief after the hubbub inside. She was healing, but the crowd and the noise inside had made her feel claustrophobic and more than a little desperate to escape. A few random raindrops tapped on the tin roof above her head.

It was peaceful here, the rhythmic squeak of the swing and the sounds of the animals drifting on the misty breeze. She could see why Garrett chose to live on the ranch with his brothers instead of in town.

The front door opened and Garrett stepped out, closing the door quickly behind him. From the look on his face, he'd felt the need to escape as keenly as she did. His eyes searched the dim porch and she could see him smile when he spotted her in the swing.

He sat down, stretching his arm out behind her. "Little too rowdy in there?"

"I don't get out much."

He barked a laugh. "Neither do they. It's why they're so loud. Plus they have a lot of kids."

"A *lot* of kids," Abby agreed. "She's ready for a burp."

As Abby handed Charlotte to Garrett, he brought her to his chest, kissed her little head and whispered something Abby couldn't hear.

The sweetness of the gesture made her throat ache and she looked away, instead watching the glimmer of raindrops in the circle from the pole light by the barn.

Patting Charlotte's back, Garrett said, "It was nice of you to come tonight."

Abby leaned back against the seat and brought one knee up to her chest, wrapping her arms around it. "Wynn made me come. She said you celebrate everything in this town."

"Yeah." His chuckle made her smile. "A lot of my friends, like Wynn, arc either foster parents or have adopted kids. When they started fostering, they realized that no one really celebrated foster babies the way they do biological babies. So they decided to make it a thing."

"It's really sweet. Every baby should be celebrated."

"I agree."

They sat in silence for a few seconds, the rhythmic squeaking of the swing and the rain on the roof making Abby feel relaxed and sleepy. "Did you always know you wanted to come back to Red Hill Springs to practice law?"

He glanced over at her with a smile. "I guess I did. Devin left home at eighteen and competed on the rodeo circuit. I went away to school, thanks to some scholarships, but I never seriously considered living anywhere else. My roots are here."

The stab of longing surprised Abby. She had no roots, not really, and there was a part of her that wondered what it would be like, what kind of deep confidence that kind of belonging would inspire.

"I sold my house in town last year. First, because we needed the money so we could hang on to the ranch and then… I guess it's not really true what they say about never going home again. My cabin was a ramshackle dump, but it felt more like home than my place in town ever had."

"You guys manage the ranch together?"

"Yep. Lacey and Devin run the farm stand, which has been way more successful than we ever thought it would be. Tanner's the one who got the farming gene." Charlotte started to fuss and Garrett shifted her to his arm.

"And you?"

"I mostly manage the finances…and raise the goats." He sent her a sideways glance, the perpetual amusement that was so much a part of him twinkling in his eyes.

"What?" She laughed softly. "I never pictured you as a goatherd."

"Oh, there's no herding involved. All I have to do is walk into the field with a box of raisins in my pocket and they'll do my bidding."

"That's hilarious. I had no idea the depth of your talents. I've eaten goat but I can't say that I've ever had any as pets," Abby mused.

He gave an exaggerated look over his shoulder. "Shh—they'll hear you."

She laughed again. "My apologies to your goats."

"They accept."

With the baby drifting back to sleep in the crook of his arm, he stretched the other one out behind her again. His fingers played with the ends of her hair, sending shivers down her back.

The rain was coming down harder now and she sighed. "I think it's settling in for the night and I've got to get back and let Elvis out. I'd love to bring him out to the farm sometime though. It's good for him to be exposed to new sights and sounds. Keeps him from being spooked when we're in the field."

"Sure If the rain clears tomorrow, bring him over. He can chase chickens." He looked down at her as she shook her head. "I mean, no, he definitely can't chase chickens because that would be...wrong."

She chuckled. "He has to completely ignore them and keep doing his job."

"Which is?"

"Making people feel safe, giving unconditional love and acceptance. And he does that with my cues, so he can't get distracted or he'll miss them."

"I saw the hand signal you gave him when Nash came in the office. Was that how he knew to go to him and lay his head on Nash's lap?"

"Yes, along with the verbal cue to 'go say hello.'"

"So, if you mostly do mental health work with kids during disaster relief, how did you and Elvis end up working in a refugee camp?" Garrett's question was innocent but it sent her edgy nerves into overdrive, her pulse skyrocketing.

She took a deep breath and tried to ground herself here, in this moment. Rain on the roof. Cool breeze against her skin. "Some people in Syria have been displaced by violence over and over again. Children are suffering. When one of the agencies I worked with in the past asked me if I'd take Elvis and do some training with their counselors there, I couldn't say no."

She waited, tension knotting between her shoulders. She was afraid of what he would ask next. Not that she was secretive, but the memories were still so raw and so painful. What if the floodgates opened and she couldn't get them closed again?

"I can't imagine how hard that must've been."

"It was very different. Even though disaster relief is hard, usually by the time I leave, I can see small signs of recovery and I know that things will continue to get better. In the refugee camp where I worked, it was harder to find things to be hopeful about. And I was there for a long time."

"How long?"

"Eight months. I was supposed to stay for a year, but after I was injured, I got sent home."

"I'm sorry." His hand dropped on her shoulder as

he rocked the swing gently, but that was it. She knew he had to have questions, but he didn't pry, didn't even make her feel bad about not sharing more.

Abby jerked upright as the front door slammed open. Latham backed out the door with a sleeping A.J. draped over his shoulder, calling back into the house. "It's pouring out here. If you'll come get her, I'll bring the car up."

Charlotte woke and started to fuss. Latham turned toward the sound and winced. "Oops, sorry, guys."

A few seconds later, Wynn came out of the open front door, followed by Penny. "Oh, there you are, Abby. Thanks for coming tonight. You're a big part of Project Help Garrett Survive."

"I don't know about that, but it was fun."

Latham handed A.J. to Wynn. "Be right back with the car. Congratulations, Garrett."

"Thanks, man."

Abby dug her keys out of her pocket, following Garrett to the top of the stairs. "I've really got to go, too."

"I'll touch base with you in the morning about bringing Elvis over," Garrett called to her as she started down the steps into the rain.

Abby tossed a wave in his general direction and ran through the downpour for her car, beeping the door locks open as she ran.

She slid into the car and slammed the door, shaking water off her hair. The conversation about her work in the refugee camp had unnerved her. She fought the urge to look in the backseat. She was safe here.

Latham pulled his car around to the porch. Abby watched as he jumped out to open the door for Penny while Wynn ducked through the rain to buckle the baby into her seat. They worked together as a unit and Abby couldn't help but feel a little envious. The family she'd had as a kid hadn't exactly prepared her for a relationship, not the kind Wynn had, anyway.

Garrett was still on the porch with Charlotte, swaying a little as he tried to get her back to sleep. His friends and family had been poking fun at him tonight, and he'd handled it in his easygoing way.

If she allowed herself a minute to wonder what it would be like if she and Garrett and Charlotte were a family, it was just normal curiosity. More than ever, she was at a crossroads in her life. Goals had to be set. Decisions made.

Her phone buzzed in the seat beside her. She picked it up. The message was from her former boss, who didn't seem to be able to accept no for an answer. In the past, Abby had willingly given up vacation, Sundays, holidays. Disasters happened without regard to what day of the week or year it was. But this time, she couldn't.

She wasn't saying never, but she was definitely saying *not right now*. She had to rebuild her resilience, and Red Hill Springs was a part of that, giving her something positive to focus on.

She'd told the truth when she said good-night to Wynn. Tonight had been a fun reprieve. But as good as it was, now that the party was over, she only felt more alone. She'd never felt like she belonged, not like that.

She was a bystander at best. This was their life.

But maybe for a little while, she would let herself pretend that it could be hers, too.

Chapter Six

The next afternoon, Garrett held Charlotte nestled in the crook of his arm. Her cheeks were rosy, her little mouth primping. She was sleeping but he didn't want to let go of her. "She had a bottle at noon, so when she wakes up she'll be hungry. I fixed a three-ounce bottle but sometimes she wants an extra ounce."

"I got it. The twins aren't so old that I don't remember the newborn stage." Lacey held out her arms for the baby.

He still didn't give her up. "She's been spitting up a little bit so I try to sit her up after she eats."

"Yep."

"There's this one rattle she likes that lights up. It's in the bag. Her favorite blanket is in there, too."

"She has a favorite blanket? She's a month…" Lacey's voice trailed off as she caught his warning look. "Favorite blanket. Got it. Garrett, you have to actually leave her if I'm going to babysit while you show Abby around the farm."

A knock on the door emphasized her words and Garrett reluctantly handed the baby over to his sister-in-law. "Are you sure you don't mind?"

"Pish. What's one more? Besides, the twins will be napping most of the time. And you'll be within shouting distance if I need you."

"I know, I know." He opened the front door to greet Abby, then stooped down to give Elvis a scratch. "You ready for a tour?"

"Definitely." After the rain, the weather had turned warmer and Abby was dressed in jeans, cheerful yellow rubber boots and a heather gray T-shirt. Her dark hair was a riot of curls with the humidity.

He smiled at her. "You look nice."

"You mean the circles under my eyes have faded from black and purple to a mere lavender?"

"No." He made a quizzical face. "I don't think that's what I meant."

"Oh, I didn't know you guys had a dog! Hello, girl." Abby's normally alto voice rose as she knelt down to greet Sadie, Tanner's rottweiler-shepherd mix. She held her hand out for a sniff before she scratched Sadie's big black head. She looked up at Garrett. "She's gorgeous. Farm dog?"

Garrett laughed. "More of a lie-by-the-fire dog. But she's smart and completely unflappable, so sometimes Devin uses her to help calm a spooky horse."

Sadie was curious about Elvis, who waited patiently as the big black dog sniffed him from nose to tail. And when Abby straightened, Sadie nudged her hand, greedy for more attention. Abby laughed and obliged her with another good scratch as she looked across the driveway to where Devin patiently circled his latest equine client. "What's going on over there?"

"Devin's gotten kind of a reputation for being able to work with problem horses, so these days we almost always have an extra boarder in the barn. He has a knack with them, probably because he was such a problem child."

"Oh, I can't believe that." Abby laughed as they walked, Sadie running ahead. She gave Elvis a hand signal which apparently gave him the freedom to leave her side because he took off, joining Sadie to romp in the wet grass along the side of the dirt road.

"His attention is always on you. Does everyone train therapy dogs like you have?"

"No, Elvis is different. He's trained to do animal-assisted therapy. His superpower is making people feel comfortable enough to talk." She stopped as they rounded a bend and a field of multicolored wildflowers stretched out as far as they could see. She breathed out an awestruck sigh. "Oh, Garrett. These are beautiful."

"We raise them to sell, but we get to enjoy them for a while first."

"They're so pretty." Abby walked into the field, letting her hands skim the tops of the flowers. She turned back, laughter in her eyes. "I'm probably not allowed to do this, but I don't care. I love how happy they are."

He pulled a folded knife from his pocket and sliced the stems of a handful of the colorful, bright blooms.

She left the field, oblivious to the mud coating her rubber boots, eyes lighting up in delight as he handed her the small bouquet. "Thank you."

"My pleasure." As she brought the fragrant blooms to her face, he caught himself wishing for simpler times.

That their lives weren't so complicated, that they were just two ordinary people who met at church or at the diner and struck up a conversation.

Deliberately, he folded his knife and slid it into his pocket before looking up again. "So, since we're here so Elvis can get some exposure to farm life, I'm curious about how you got started doing...what you do."

The sun was weak but welcome as it dappled the ground in front of them. She walked a few steps beside him down the gravel road. "My master's is in trauma and crisis counseling. I started out on a volunteer team while I was doing my training and eventually transitioned into full time."

"That easy, huh?"

"Yep. I guess you could say I stumbled into my calling."

Garrett stopped next to the pasture fence. Elvis loped toward them, circled Abby and then ran back to join Sadie. "How long have you had Elvis?"

"Five years. He was a game changer. Kids love him and maybe they don't want to tell some strange lady something, but they'll tell Elvis."

"I saw him with Nash. He's amazing."

"He's a natural." Abby gave a low whistle and, even though Elvis was roughhousing with Sadie, his head came up immediately. He trotted back to her side and dropped into place. She discreetly slipped him a treat. "Regardless of what's going on, he has to stay calm and obedient."

"Like when there are strange dogs or loud roosters or goats?"

"Exactly." She laughed. "It's funny, but it really helps."

He paused at the end of the lane, where the path

forked. "To the left is the pond. It's spring fed, so it's around fifty-four degrees even in the middle of the summer. It was great when we were kids. My dad would make us work in the fields and barn and we would sweat and complain. But then late in the afternoon, we'd go swimming in the pond. My mom would bring us frozen pops and sit in the chair with her book, trying not to get wet."

A smile curved her lips. "It sounds like fun."

"It was." At least until his mom died and everything fell apart. And then it hadn't been fun at all. He took a deep breath. "My cabin's just over the hill to the right."

"Oh, wow." Her voice was pensive. "Charlotte's mom had to walk a long way to drop her off. I wonder what she was thinking. If she was scared. How desperate she must've felt, but also maybe, how hopeful."

He glanced over at her. Her eyes were a little misty and he could tell she was thinking about Brooklyn and what she must've been going through to make the choice to leave her baby behind. Most people would judge, but Abby didn't. "How do you do that?"

"What?"

"See things from the other person's point of view so easily? Most people are horrified that Brooklyn abandoned her baby."

"That's valid, too. But people do things for all kinds of reasons that we don't understand if we haven't been in their shoes. And we really have no idea what she was thinking and feeling."

"I've been texting her a photo every day. So far no response, though." He turned back toward the barn and the house and the dogs followed, bounding around them.

"Have you asked her to contact you again?" Abby tapped her hip and Elvis fell into step beside her.

"Not yet." He shrugged. "I want her to feel like her wishes have been respected, I guess. I don't know. I'm honestly flying blind here."

"It seems like your instincts are good. I wish I'd met her."

"I wish she'd had the chance to talk to you. Maybe she will one day." As they made their way back toward the house, he stopped in the middle of the lane. "What next? We have a new litter of kittens in the barn."

She held both hands up. "Uh-uh. I can't resist fluffy baby kitties with their tiny pink noses and scratchy little tongues."

Garrett stifled a laugh. "Yeah, that's how I got Thelma and Louise. They were each the size of a big puppy when I got them, and so feisty and cute. Irresistible. The kittens aren't ready to leave their mom yet if that makes you feel any better."

"It totally does. I'm dying to see them." She looked up at him, eyes sparkling under her dark lashes. "No matter what I say, promise me you won't let me get a kitten."

She disappeared into the barn.

Garrett stood, feet rooted, in the middle of the drive.

He was no stranger to trauma. He'd been through it himself. He'd seen it in countless clients—adults and children—that he'd worked with over the years. He recognized it in Abby, too.

But today, he was seeing glimpses of who she was without it, and she was stunning. He pressed his fingers into his forehead. His timing could not be worse. "Get it together, Garrett."

Abby poked her head back out the barn door. "Did you say something?"

"Nope. Not a thing." He shook his head and followed her into the barn.

Abby stopped in the doorway to let her eyes adjust to the dim space. She stood in a shotgun building with doors at either end of a long hall. The floor was dirt and the walls full of cracks, but it smelled of fresh hay and farm animals.

Garrett appeared at her elbow, his voice low. "We've got plans to build a new barn so Devin can expand his horse business."

She looked up at him. "I like this one."

"Me, too." He pointed to the stall in the back of the barn that was next to the partially open doors leading to the round pen where Devin had been working the horse earlier.

At the back of the stall, tucked into a corner, was a gray striped kitty with four little kittens—one gray tabby, two orange and one calico—in tumbled disarray around her. Abby melted. "Oh, they're so sweet. Is it okay if I get closer?"

"Sure."

She dropped to her knees and got a sleepy stare from the mama kitty, but no other signs of alarm. "When did their eyes open?"

"Just yesterday. A couple of them have started exploring but they don't get far before they fall over and have to take a nap."

Abby picked up the calico baby and gently rubbed

its tiny forehead as she cupped the kitten in her hands. She laughed. "This was such a mistake. I love this one."

The mother cat had shaken herself loose, literally, from the babies and rubbed her head against the leg of Garrett's jeans. He rubbed her head. "Mrs. Smith is the best barn cat we've ever had. She runs a tight ship around here."

Abby smiled. "You have working animals around this farm. Sadie helps Devin with training. Mrs. Smith keeps the barn tidy."

"Devin's horse Reggie is one of the best cow horses in the country."

She lifted a shoulder. "There you go. The idea of animals having jobs that help humans is nothing new around here."

"Point taken. It's not so weird to have a partner that's a dog after all."

The cat, who'd been the picture of feline adoration, stretched her paws up Garrett's legs and stabbed him with her claws. He yelped.

"That is why you're not allowed in the house." He scowled at Mrs. Smith, who primly made her way back to her kittens and flopped down.

Elvis nosed his way into the barn. Abby smiled. "Hey fella, you having fun?"

He stuck his nose into the curve of her neck where she cuddled the kitten, and snorted. She obliged him with a good long sniff of the strange-smelling thing she was holding.

"Wish my life was in a spot where I could adopt her. She's so cute. I would name her Frances Perkins after the first woman who was on a president's cabinet. She was a social worker."

"Well, Frances it is, then."

Abby kissed the kitten on the nose and reluctantly returned her to her mom. Maybe one day.

She stood and brushed the hay from her pants, putting her hand on a ladder as she stepped out into the breezeway again. "What's up there?"

"I'll show you if you're feeling adventurous."

"Am I going to fall through the floor?"

His laugh filled the barn, as well as some of the dark spaces in her that hadn't heard laughter in a long time. She crossed her arms. "I'm guessing that's why this is an adventure? Because my life might be in danger?"

His eyes, dark and a little serious, met hers. "I wouldn't let anything happen to you, Abby."

Because she believed him and because her heart seemed to suddenly be beating erratically, she motioned for Elvis to stay and took the first step onto the ladder.

At the top, Garrett reached around her and threw open a small window. From this vantage point, she could see for miles. What had seemed like flat farmland was really a series of rolling hills. Streams and creeks were dark slashes in shades of green. The spring-fed ponds that the area was known for gleamed in the distance.

"It's breathtaking, Garrett. I had no idea."

He sat down against a post. Warm afternoon light speared into the space, making the dust seem like tiny sparkling fairies. "When my dad was alive, he always seemed to be surrounded by a halo of dust. Dusty boots, dusty hat. He'd appear in the door of the barn in the late afternoon and he'd just be a silhouette."

Abby sat beside him, looking up at the square of blue sky that showed in the window he'd opened. "He must've been an amazing man to raise three sons who turned out like you and Devin and Tanner."

He snorted. "We've all had our moments, believe me, but he was amazing. He wasn't a big talker—Tanner takes after him, I think—but he was always teaching us. How to take care of the land. How to be a man. How to love a woman. He loved my mom so much."

She swallowed hard but he didn't notice. His eyes were on the beams of sunlight.

"My mom, on the other hand, always seemed to be bathed in sunlight. She'd come out onto the porch in the evening and hold her hand up to shade her eyes. When I think about her, she always seems golden."

"You miss them."

"I'd gotten used to not thinking about them but then, I'm sitting there holding this baby, trying to figure out how to be a dad…" His voice trailed off. The corner of his mouth tipped up. "After my mom died, I used to come up here in the afternoon and watch those beams of light walk across the floor. They'd slide across my skin and I'd pretend it was a message from my mom, that she was touching me from up in the sky."

Her throat ached, thinking about him as a young boy, needing his parents, missing them.

"How old were you?" Her voice, though it was quiet, seemed loud in the space.

He looked at her then, the smile lines crinkling around his eyes. "Fourteen. Devin was twelve and he needed parenting. Tanner had lost his wife and baby, but he did his best to be there for Devin."

"Who was there for you?" She could feel the ache in his words and she was afraid she knew the answer.

"Everyone was grieving so hard." He held his hand out, letting the sunlight filter through his fingers. "I just kept my head down and tried not to make any trouble. Devin made enough for both of us."

The smile was back.

She said, "Oh, Garrett."

"When Mom and Dad died, I felt like I might never be put back together. But I kept coming up here and looking at those beams. I didn't even know why. But then one day I realized that without all the cracks in the walls, the light wouldn't be able to get in. The beauty of the sunlight comes from the cracks."

His hand brushed hers, sending electric shocks up her arm. Tension stretched but it was like a tight string between the two of them. It scared her a little how much she wanted to reach for him, comfort him.

In the distance, a screen door slammed and a thin wail rose. Garrett stood with a laugh and held his hand out to her. "Wow, I brought you up here to show you the view, not to tell you all my adolescent secrets."

Grasping his hand, she let him pull her to her feet, wincing as the healing wound in her side stretched. She followed him down the ladder, pausing almost imperceptibly when his hands gripped her waist to steady her as she stepped off the last rung.

On solid ground, she looked up. His face was inches away, his eyes warm on hers. He whispered, "Abby."

She knew he was about to kiss her. As if a breath of air nudged her, she moved closer.

Garrett reached up and brushed a piece of hair away from her face, his touch achingly gentle.

Elvis bumped her leg, grounding her in reality. Abby

took a step back, one hand moving in a hidden hand gesture to Elvis, who wedged his way between them, creating space.

"Were you wondering where she went, boy?" Garrett laughed and gave Elvis a good scratch, the moment gone so quickly Abby almost wondered if she'd imagined it.

As they stepped out of the barn, fat raindrops started to fall, splattering on the ground. Garrett squinted up at the sky. "I guess that's the end of our sunny day. Want to come in for something to drink?"

Dark clouds were gathering in the west. It was tempting to extend the time she'd spent with him today. It was easy to be with him, easy to feel close to him. But for him, doing that was just part of who he was—he gave his best to everyone.

For her, it was starting to feel a little too personal. Too important.

So Abby shook her head. "Thanks, but I need to be getting back."

"It was fun showing you around. Next time, you'll have to meet the goats and we'll ride if you want to."

He lifted his hat and ran his fingers through his hair, looking down at his dusty boots, and she wavered. But she knew there probably wouldn't be a next time. There was a good chance she wouldn't be here much longer. This attraction she felt to Garrett was just that, a temporary attachment. To believe anything else would be setting herself up for heartache.

And she had enough of that already.

Chapter Seven

"Hey, is Garrett in yet?" Abby stopped at Bess's desk on her way to her office. "I think I was supposed to watch Charlotte this morning."

"Nope." Bess looked up with a smile, her light brown hair in one long braid over her shoulder, fingers pausing on the keyboard. "Haven't heard from him but he's got court in less than an hour."

"Do you think I should text him?"

"Already did. I'll let you know if I hear from him." The executive assistant's eyes were back on her screen.

"Thanks, Bess." Abby walked back to her office. She pulled her cell phone out of her purse but there was no message from Garrett.

Sitting down at her desk, she opened her laptop, glanced at the time on the screen and back at the empty office. She'd caught a glimpse of Garrett at church yesterday but he had to leave early and she didn't get a chance to talk to him. She couldn't stop thinking about that moment in the barn Saturday afternoon. Had she imagined the connection between them?

Was she the only one who felt it?

Was thinking about this a total waste of her time? Yeah, she knew the answer to that question.

Abby blinked her eyes and forced them to focus on the computer screen. She'd had a very promising meeting with the counselors from the local schools early this morning. They'd been excited by the possibility of referring families to her for counseling and support, so she wanted to send them a follow-up email while the meeting was fresh in their minds.

The front door opened. Finally. She listened for Garrett's voice, but all she could hear was Charlotte screaming. Oh, boy. She closed her laptop and walked to the door of her office, swallowing a gasp as she took in his appearance.

He looked awful—eyes red-rimmed, skin tinged with gray, hair standing on end. "What's going on? Are you okay?"

"Were you at church yesterday?"

"Yeah. I saw you get the nursery SOS." She reached for the infant carrier and placed it on her desk. Charlotte's face was red, eyes squinched shut, her tiny lips trembling with each new cry.

"She's barely stopped since. The only time she slows down is if I'm holding her *while* I'm standing up." He rubbed his eyes and blinked at Abby wearily. "She can be dead asleep and if I sit down, she starts up again."

"No wonder you look tired."

"I have a court appearance—" he flipped his wrist over to glance at his watch "—right now, and then a couple of meetings, but I'll be back as soon as I can. Sorry to leave you with her like this."

"It's okay." Abby had to raise her voice to hear her own words over Charlotte's loud wails. "Did you call Ash?"

"Texted. He said sometimes babies cry and if she starts running a fever or gets lethargic to bring her in. In other words, not helpful at all." He had his keys in hand as he backed toward the door. "She had her last bottle an hour ago."

"Got it." Abby rocked the seat back and forth, but Charlotte's cries never wavered. "Don't worry, we'll be fine."

Garrett looked skeptical but he grabbed his briefcase from his office and walked out the door, clipping the door frame with his shoulder on the way out. Oh, man. She said a quick prayer that he made it to his appointments in one piece.

Charlotte, all ten pounds of her, was trembling and sweaty and mad as a hornet. Abby unbuckled her and lifted her out, holding the tiny body gently as she bounced up and down. "Oh my goodness, little girl. You're all worked up."

The question in Abby's mind was *why*? She ran through a mental checklist of things that could be bothering Charlotte. Hungry? No, Garrett said she'd eaten an hour earlier. Wet? Maybe.

Abby grabbed the diaper bag and carried Charlotte into the bathroom and laid her on the changing table, trying not to wince as the crying intensified. "Hang on, Charlotte, let's just see what's up."

She started with baby's head and closely examined every inch to make sure Charlotte didn't have an insect bite or scratchy clothing tag or something bothering her, but she saw nothing. Not even a little diaper rash. Was it possible she was itchy? Allergic to the detergent Garrett used to wash her clothes?

Iffy, considering she'd had no reaction before, but Abby pulled a thin muslin blanket from the drawer of clothes Garrett kept here for emergencies. Placing Charlotte in the center of it, she tucked the blanket around the baby until she was completely swaddled.

For the next forty-five minutes, Abby walked in circles around her office. Charlotte would take the pacifier and act like she was sleepy, only to spit it out and start fussing again moments later.

Abby tried holding her in different positions. She tried walking outside. She even tried laying Charlotte down in the porta-crib in Garrett's office and letting her be. Nothing seemed to appease the normally easygoing infant.

Wynn opened the office door. "*What* is going on? I could hear her screaming when I came in the front door."

"According to Garrett, she's been crying like this since he picked her up from the nursery at church yesterday."

Wynn shrugged. "I don't know. Have you tried feeding her? Could be a growth spurt."

Abby's phone buzzed on the desk: a phone call from Garrett. She looked down at Charlotte. "It's your dad. You're gonna need to be quiet for a second."

Charlotte didn't look convinced. She didn't sound convinced either, letting out another loud cry.

"Let me have her while you answer the phone."

Wynn took Charlotte and Abby ducked out of the office, closing the door behind her.

"Hello?"

"Hey, I was just calling to check and see if she was any better, but I can hear her."

Abby glanced back to where Wynn was swaying back and forth with Charlotte. "Yeah, she's still not happy. I've tried everything I can think of. It's a little early, but I was about to give her a bottle."

"I wonder if we should just take her to the doctor."

We? "How about this? I saw the thermometer in her bag. I'll take her temperature and if she's running a fever, I'll call and make an appointment. If not, I'll just give her a bottle and we'll go from there."

"Did I put a thermometer in her diaper bag?"

"Yep. It's in the same little zipper pouch as the infant acetaminophen."

"Okay, good plan. Oh, hang on." She heard rustling and muffled voices and then Garrett's voice came back. "They're calling our case. I'll get back there as soon as I can. Thanks, Abby."

The phone went silent.

When she opened the door to the office, Wynn handed Charlotte back. "She definitely doesn't want me. Should I fix her a bottle?"

"That would be great." As she spoke, Abby realized she could hear herself. She looked down. Charlotte had gone silent and was staring intently at her face, more alert than Abby had ever seen her.

Then the little bottom lip poked out and Abby's eyes went wide. "No, don't do that. No, no, no. Aunt Wynn is getting the bottle, I promise."

A few minutes later, Abby settled in the chair with Charlotte and the bottle, which seemed—fingers crossed—to be doing the trick.

Abby wedged the bottle between her chin and the baby and picked up the thermometer. Thankfully, she just had to run it over Charlotte's forehead to check her temperature. The screen flashed green. Ninety-nine.

So no fever to speak of. Charlotte's eyes were closed and she didn't notice when Abby removed the bottle. Easing a limp-noodle newborn into position on her shoulder without waking her up was easier said than done, but she did it. She leaned back against the seat with a sigh of relief as she patted the little back.

Wow. That hour had been intense, and poor Garrett had experienced nearly twenty-four hours of that. No wonder he looked shell-shocked.

Wynn paused outside the closed door and gave Abby a thumbs-up.

Abby returned a wan smile and let her head drop back against the seat. She picked it up as her phone buzzed again. Expecting Garrett, she was surprised to see her boss's name pop up on the home screen. Her thumb hesitated over the notification. There'd been a time when she would've been excited to see the name, ready to grab her go-bag and head for the airport at a moment's notice. Her work was important and she'd loved it.

Five years later, she'd been tired, but still, she'd believed in the difference she made with kids who'd lost everything. She'd believed until her time in the refugee camp. Rationally, she knew that she'd helped in a small way, that the children she and Elvis worked with knew someone cared about what they had gone through.

Her heart—that was a different story. Her heart said the hours she spent with the kids couldn't stack up when it came to what those little people had been through. It wasn't just losing their homes, or losing their families. Or the abuse that happened in so many forms. It wasn't the absence of the familiar. Or a life-changing injury.

In some cases, it was *all* of that combined. She'd given them everything she had. She'd almost given her life and still, she didn't feel like it was enough.

With a quick flick of her thumb across the screen, Abby opened the phone and read the text from Greta. I know we said six months…

Abby wanted to laugh because her vacations, such as they were, always ended early. But this time, she couldn't make that happen. She'd stepped away from a precipice when she'd given her notice. And this time it wasn't as simple as canceling hotel reservations.

She had responsibilities here

In her arms, Charlotte gave a quivering sigh. Abby rubbed the tiny back and put her phone aside. So many things were up in the air for her right now, but she'd always been a person who'd given her best to every moment of her day. And right now, that meant being here for Charlotte.

Garrett stepped into the office, stopping with his hand on the doorknob, phone to his ear. "No, I'm not happy with status quo. I don't want a continuance. This family deserves permanence and I don't want to wait three more months to give it to them."

Somewhere in the back, he heard the baby start to cry. He closed his eyes. "I have to go."

Garrett's head was pounding. His feet felt like they weighed two tons and he just wanted to lie down somewhere. But he had other responsibilities now. He pushed the door closed and turned around to find Bess with noise-canceling headphones on. Smart.

In his office, he found Abby pacing the floor with Charlotte. "Still at it, I see."

"Well, she was sleeping until you started shouting as you came in the door."

"I wasn't shouting. I was getting my point across." He scowled at Abby. "Why doesn't she have any clothes on? She's probably crying because she's cold."

"She's not cold. It's seventy-two degrees in here, thank you."

Garrett pressed the fingers of both hands against his temples. "No one's getting any work done anyway. I'll just take her home."

"Hey, guys." The voice startled both of them and the pitch of Charlotte's cries grew louder.

How was that even possible?

Ash Sheehan stepped into Garrett's office. "My sister told me if Charlotte was still fussy that I should stop by on my way back to the office from the hospital."

Garrett said, "She's still fussy."

"She slept for about forty-five minutes, until Garrett got here. Now she's crying again." Abby followed Ash into the main office with Charlotte in her arms.

Ash set his bag on the conference table and walked to Abby, with his hands out. "May I?"

Crooning softly, the pediatrician held Charlotte face

down, folding her arms against her body. As her arms stopped flailing, her frantic cries tapered off.

Garrett stared at Ash. "What kind of mind control am I seeing here?"

"Nothing like that. Just experience." When Ash wiggled her legs a little bit with his other hand, Charlotte's breath hitched, but she stopped crying. Ash looked at Garrett. "How old is she?"

He blanked. "Uh…"

"Five weeks." Abby didn't even glance at Garrett as she answered. And he deserved it. He'd been a jerk.

"I learned this trick from one of my pediatric attendings. I don't know why it works, but it always does." Ash moved from the leg jiggle to a slow, rolling bounce. Charlotte's eyes were open, her mottled color returning to normal baby pink. He held Charlotte out to Garrett. "You try."

After an awkward transfer, Garrett copied the hand position and movement he'd seen Ash do and it worked for him, too. The supersecret-pediatrician baby hold wouldn't help the not-sleeping situation, but at least maybe he'd be able to calm her down.

Ash nodded his approval. "Good, you got it. Okay, so here's what you need to know. Five weeks is one of those times when you can get a double whammy with newborns. They're growing so fast that sometimes they need extra feedings or to have the amount of formula increased."

Abby nodded. "I gave her an extra bottle this morning and it seemed to help."

"The second thing is what some call Wonder Weeks. You might notice that she's holding eye contact better. She may get more control of her head. Stretch out her sleeping time at night. Stuff like that. New parents call us all the time saying their easygoing baby is inconsolable. A few days later, that baby will roll over or start crawling or say their first words. And then they're like, *oh*..."

Abby shrugged and met Garrett's eyes. "I did notice she was very alert this morning. Maybe there's something to this."

"There is something to it, trust me." Ash reached in his bag and pulled out an instrument that Garrett recognized as the thing doctors use to look in ears. The doctor checked Charlotte's ears, took the cover off and used the light to check her throat and then asked Garrett to lay her down. After he listened to her heart and felt her belly, he draped his stethoscope around his neck. "I don't think there's anything to worry about, but you can always bring her in if things don't get better."

Abby scooped Charlotte up. "I'll change her diaper."

Garrett walked Ash to the door. "I appreciate you coming by. I know it's not normally part of the service."

Ash raised one smooth brow. "You need to take a nap. Charlotte's fine but you look like day-old stew someone left out all night."

"Yeah. I'm aware."

"All right then, see you Saturday at the Winter Carnival?"

"Sure." Garrett closed the door behind Ash. If he was actually able to break away for the carnival, he'd probably end up napping on a blanket while the party went on around him. This newborn thing wasn't for the weak. He sighed.

For now, though, he had a more pressing duty. Turning to Abby, he noted that she had put clothes on Charlotte, which made him feel worse. "I'm sorry I was a jerk."

With the baby on her shoulder, she shoved a few ibuprofen across the surface of the table. "I'm going to drive you home so you can take a nap. Get rid of your headache and then we can talk."

He wanted to argue but he felt so horrible that he just did what she said. He took the ibuprofen. He let Abby drive him home. He pulled his tie off and dropped it on the floor before falling face-first onto his bed, asleep before he even closed his eyes.

Two hours later, he woke up with a start, not sure where he was. He squinted at the window. The sun was low in the sky, sending stripes of light through the blinds. He took stock of himself.

Headache down to a dull roar.

Body aches almost gone.

Court case still a nightmare.

Baby girl…quiet?

He smoothed the cover of the bed into place before walking out to the family room. Abby was in his oversized chair, her feet propped on the ottoman, with the sleeping baby on her chest. It was a punch in the gut to see her there, comforting the baby that he'd somehow claimed as his own.

Abby was beautiful, but it wasn't her beauty that drew him. It was her generosity, even after he'd showed his worst side. She had her eyes closed and at first, he thought she was asleep, but every once in a while, her hand moved on Charlotte's back. She was tired too, fighting emotional and physical exhaustion, the very reason she was in Red Hill Springs to begin with.

She opened her eyes and looked straight at him.

He smiled, despite the nagging feeling of guilt. "How long has she been out?"

"Almost as long as you have. But she's going to need a bottle soon."

"I'll make it." He crossed to the kitchen counter. "Thanks for letting me sleep. I feel almost human."

"What happened today?" she asked softly.

"One of the lawyers didn't show up for court, so instead of my client getting her kids back, they have to wait three more months. Three more months of the kids being in foster care when they could be with their parents. It's maddening." He went through the motions of making the bottle, everything second nature to him now. At least this one thing was easy.

"I'm sorry, Garrett."

"I'll never stop getting mad about stuff like this, but usually I handle it better than I did today. I think the situation with Charlotte and not being able to find her mom is stressing me out more than I thought it was."

"That's understandable. Have you heard from her?"

"Brooklyn? No. Every day I text her and hope this will be the day she responds. And every day I'm disappointed."

He looked at Charlotte, who was still completely tuckered out. "I'll take her. I'm sure you're ready to go home. You can drive my car back to the office. I'll get Devin to chauffeur me to work tomorrow."

Abby didn't say anything, just handed the baby to him. Charlotte squirmed, but her eyes stayed firmly shut. Probably saving up her energy to keep him awake tonight.

He touched Abby's arm. "I really am sorry. I was a jerk about the clothes. I guess all new parents get cranky with each other."

Her eyes went wide and he realized—and immediately regretted—that he'd made it sound like *they* were the parents.

"It's fine, Garrett. I know you've had a rough couple of days." She stayed at arm's length, but gave him a too-bright smile as she opened the door. "Okay, hope you two have a better night. Just shoot me a text if you need a ride in the morning."

He stopped. "Abby…"

"I'll see you tomorrow." She closed the door, leaving him standing there staring at it, more confused than ever about what to do next. What happened to the effortless communication they'd seemed to have in the barn?

His brothers teased him about how easily he fell in love, but what he'd felt on Saturday wasn't just attraction or infatuation. It had seemed real and deep. And he wondered if she felt the same way.

Maybe it was just him.

By the time he'd finished feeding Charlotte her bottle, he'd decided the best—and only—course of action was to pretend the awkward conversation never happened.

Chapter Eight

Abby didn't hear from Garrett the next day or the next, other than a quick text to let her know that he was working at home. She had an uneasy feeling that the "new parent" comment had messed up the easy relationship they'd built. Surely he hadn't meant to imply anything except that other people with babies probably dealt with conflict. Crying babies were stressful.

Ugh. It had been so awkward.

Worse, she missed him. *Them*. She missed *them*.

Yesterday after work, she'd ended up walking up and down the aisles of the drugstore in bored desperation and had spent her evening trying various colored face masks, which she was completely convinced were overrated. Her skin was not glowing and poreless, thank you very much.

She'd tried reading but couldn't concentrate, all of which made her wonder if maybe she should consider her boss's offer to come back to work. So when Wynn asked if Abby wanted to meet up at the park for a walk Thursday morning, she'd jumped on the offer.

Unfortunately, she'd forgotten how out of shape she was.

"What is bugging you? You've barely said two words to me since we got here." Beside her, Wynn was walking at a brisk pace, elbows pumping, ponytail swinging.

Abby wasn't sure she could breathe, much less talk, but she tried. "I'm fine. Why aren't you working today?"

"Most of the time, I only take the cases I really want to take and the rest of the time, I work as the mayor. I'll be in the office to meet with clients this afternoon. Then tomorrow I'll be helping to get things ready for the Winter Carnival on Saturday. The vendors start setting up at daylight."

"What's the Winter Carnival?" Abby wheezed out the words. Her lungs were burning. She couldn't feel her legs anymore.

Wynn shot her a sideways glance and slowed the pace—marginally. "You'll love it. We have all kinds of food trucks and craft sellers and bouncy houses for the kids. Bands playing all day. It's really fun...as long as it doesn't rain."

"Is it supposed to?"

"As of an hour ago, there was a forty percent chance, but I don't even want to think about that. Let's talk about you and Garrett instead."

Despite years of practice at keeping a noncommittal expression, Abby was sure her inner feelings were broadcast over her face. She stopped walking, hands on her hips as she sucked in air. "There is no me and Garrett. He's already...oh, never mind. I'm helping with the baby just like everyone else, and that's all."

Wynn slowed to a stop and paced back to Abby, concern in her blue eyes. "I touched a nerve. I'm sorry. I blunder in sometimes without thinking first. But, honey, you know you can talk to me about anything. I care about you."

Abby sighed, turned Wynn back to the path and started walking beside her. Slowly. "I'm sorry, too. I'm just on edge. I am worried that I might've messed things up with Garrett. And on top of that, my boss keeps pressuring me to come back."

Wynn walked in silence for a few seconds. "Let's table the Garrett discussion and talk about that last thing. Are you going to?"

"Go back? No. I made the decision that was best for me." Abby paused, trying to think how to put into words what she was feeling. "There's a point when you've been dealing with trauma for so long that all the intense emotions start to feel normal. Your body can't live in a heightened state for months or years on end—it's just not possible."

"And that's what happened in Syria?"

Their path wound past the playground. Little kids were playing tag and squealing with laughter. A couple of moms pushed their babies in the swings. And across the green field, there was a group of people doing yoga in the park.

It was peaceful. Happy. What normal *should* be like. "In a way. I lost my sense of fear and went into an area I shouldn't have been in. Trusted someone I shouldn't have trusted." She shook her head and sighed again. It all still felt so heavy. "I have to find my baseline again."

"You're welcome to stay, you know that." Wynn's

expression was hopeful as she sent Abby a sideways glance.

A laugh, the release of the pent-up tension, burst out. "You really are relentless, aren't you?"

"I might have heard that a time or two." Wynn shrugged with a laugh. "But listen, this is important. Any decision you make doesn't have to be an either-or thing. You can still make a difference even if you don't go back to traveling the world."

Abby's eyes filled and she looked away, across the park. The words felt like what she'd been waiting to hear, which seemed silly. She was an adult and didn't need anyone's permission to make decisions.

Still.

Wynn's voice softened. "I know a little bit about this battle. Changing the world doesn't have to be on a large scale. Because with every single thing you do, you have the power to change one person's world."

"I guess I feel like I'm giving up. Running away."

Wynn stopped walking and faced her. "Don't take this the wrong way, okay?"

Abby crossed her arms with a sigh. "When someone says, 'Don't get offended,' that's usually a sign you're about to be offended."

"Okay, you're right." Wynn laughed. "But seriously. Is it possible you've *been* running all this time and now it's time to stop? I know from experience that children right here in my hometown need people willing to wade into trauma with them. People who can help them see there's more to life than just survival. You and Elvis could do that."

Despite her vow to not get offended, Abby felt the

words hit home. She stepped off the path to let a jogger pass them, and took a calming breath. "That's definitely something to consider. Thank you for being honest with me."

"I'm sorry." Wynn put her arm around Abby and steered them both back to the path. "I know it's hard. Believe me."

It was hard. Hard to think about giving up the thing that she'd felt defined her for so many years, but maybe Wynn was right. Maybe work, with its emotional demands and need for constant travel, had given her a convenient excuse to not build ties.

She'd known from an early age that it hurt when bonds with people were broken. It didn't take a genius to figure out that her mother's rejection had created a deep mistrust within her. So maybe Wynn was right that she'd used work to keep other people at a distance. Maybe even to escape conversations like the one she needed to have with Garrett.

Helping other people through their pain and fear came easily for her.

Facing her own fear?

Not so easy at all.

With Charlotte asleep in the swing beside him, Garrett studied the plan he'd put together for the case he was trying on Monday. The witness list was complete. His line of questions for each of his witnesses and each of the witnesses from the other side made sense.

He heard a little sigh from Charlotte, but when he glanced over, she was still sleeping soundly. The growth spurt—or whatever it had been—seemed to be over, at least this time around. And taking these few days to really get her on a solid schedule was the best thing he could've done for his sanity.

Unfortunately, it did nothing for the fact that he missed seeing Abby. Which was weird, in itself. In just a month, she'd become a part of his life that he *missed*. If he didn't know better, he'd think he was actually falling for her. Was it possible that just when he'd stopped looking, the woman he'd been looking for walked into his life?

Even if it was, the panicked look on her face when he'd said they were "new parents" indicated she probably wasn't feeling the same way.

Garrett dragged his thoughts back to work. His strategy was strong. He just needed to go through the files one more time over the weekend to make sure he had all the moving pieces straight in his mind before he headed into court. Well, that, and pray everyone showed up, which seemed to be as big a problem in family court as anything else.

As he was putting his files back into the accordion folder he took to court, he heard a soft knock at the front door. He glanced at his watch. He wasn't expecting anyone.

He took a peek at Charlotte, who was still sleeping, and crossed to the door. When he pulled it open, he saw Abby heading down the stairs, back toward the farmhouse. "Hey, where are you going?"

"Oh, you're here." She stopped and slowly turned around, a blush rising on her cheeks. "I dropped by because I wanted to make sure we were okay, but then I figured if you wanted to see me, you would've."

A bright turquoise umbrella formed a halo around her head. She had on some kind of flowy floral shirt with her jeans and those bright yellow rain boots. She looked like sunshine.

"Come on in. I've got some coffee on." He held the door open. "I should warn you, it's kind of a mess in here."

Abby folded her umbrella and set it beside the door, but when she caught sight of his paper-strewn dining room table, she faltered to a stop. "You're working. I really should go."

"You're here. Please stay for coffee?"

She slid her hands down the front of her jeans, a nervous gesture that seemed so out of place with her normally serene personality. "Water, please?"

"I have water." In the kitchen, he pulled a clean glass out of the dishwasher and filled it with ice, while she stopped to steal a look at Charlotte, who was still asleep. "So what's up? How's your day been?"

"Fine. I went for a walk in the park with Wynn. Red Hill Springs is so pretty. I understand why you guys like living here."

"It's a nice place to live. I appreciate it more now that I'm older. Everyone knowing my business doesn't bother me as much." He added water to the glass from his filter system and slid it across the counter to her.

She took a sip and wandered the room. It didn't take long. "I like the flowered couch. It's you."

He smirked at her. "It was free. Also my mom's. When we were kids, it was in her sitting room where we boys were never allowed to barge in. I get a kick out of thinking how mad she would be that I put my feet on her coffee table and drink juice while I'm sitting on her yellow couch."

"I'm sure she'd be happy you're using it." Abby stopped beside him, placed her glass on the island countertop and drew in a deep breath. "I'm sorry about the other afternoon. I was bossy and we were both stressed about Charlotte crying."

"No, I'm sorry about what I said. Like we were Mom and Dad or something…"

"It's fine. I just don't want there to be something weird hanging between us. I don't have many people in my life that I care about, but I do care about you. And Charlotte, of course." Her cheeks were pink again, words tumbling out in awkward succession.

Garrett looked into her pretty hazel eyes, so full of consternation. Later he could wonder why he'd been so bold. Why he didn't just tell her it was no big deal and move on. But right now he wasn't thinking. Instead, he put his hands on her waist, tugged her forward into his arms and settled his mouth on hers, stopping the words with his lips.

Tension trembled through her before she relaxed, her lips curving under his, her eyes drifting closed. He banded one arm around her waist, sliding the other hand into the hair at the nape of her neck.

Her lips were soft and warm and, as she melted into him, his only thought was: Why had he waited so long to kiss her?

She pulled back, blinked a few times and raised an eyebrow. "You didn't have to kiss me to make me feel better."

Her subtle humor slayed him. She could easily have

chosen to smack him instead. "You really have no idea how beautiful you are, do you?"

"What? No." She stepped back. "Stop that, Garrett. You're about to make things weird again."

He leaned back against the island and crossed his arms to keep from pulling her back into his embrace. "Probably. But I like you and I feel good when I'm with you, like things are going to be okay. It was unfortunate phrasing the other day, but I can't say I haven't been thinking what it would be like between us if we were more than just friends."

"Really? I haven't done this—" She made a vague motion toward the two of them. "I *don't* do this. When I didn't hear from you, I don't know… I guess I thought I'd been mistaken about what I was feeling." She shoved a hand into her hair. "Ugh, this is so awkward."

He was an idiot and he needed to fix this. "Abby, I like you. I don't know what this is either, but I'd like to follow through and see. If that's okay with you."

"It's okay." A hint of a smile deepened the dimple at the corner of her mouth and he wanted to kiss her again. Somehow, though, that seemed like it would be crossing a line that he didn't know how to get back from. He'd already done the two-step on that line as it was.

"I should've called you. After you left, I decided that if I'm going to survive this, Charlotte needs to be on a schedule."

"Did it work?" Her eyes were twinkling now.

"Ah, yes and no. She's eating on a schedule. Sleeping, not so much."

"I should go and let you get back to your work while she's napping. Let me know if there's anything I can do."

Garrett walked with her to the door and picked up her umbrella to hand it to her. "Go to the Winter Festival with us on Saturday? There's music and the food is amazing. It'll be fun if the rain holds off."

She nodded. "I'd love that. See you Saturday."

He closed the door gently behind her and let his forehead drop against it. What had he been thinking? Neither one of them was the type for casual kissing. Abby seemed tough, but she'd been through a lot. The last thing he wanted to do was add to her pain.

His watch buzzed on his wrist, the reminder to make Charlotte's bottle for the upcoming feeding. In the kitchen, he pulled the formula can down from the cabinet and scooped the chalky powder into the bottle.

Garrett sighed. He did like her a lot, but her assignment here was temporary. And suddenly, he wasn't worried so much about breaking her heart.

Maybe he needed to keep an eye on his own.

Chapter Nine

Garrett walked alongside the stroller as Abby pushed Charlotte. There was a throng of people around them but he was hyperaware of Abby's presence, his mind reliving the moment in his kitchen when they kissed.

She, at least, seemed to be enjoying the Winter Carnival. She'd already bought goat's milk soap that smelled like lavender and vanilla, a print of the main street in Red Hill Springs and a piece of pound cake, and they'd only been here an hour.

Garrett squinted up at the sky. Its heavy gray color looked a little ominous, but so far the rain was holding off.

The band was playing country music covers and Abby sang along as they walked. He scowled, half-convinced she was driving him crazy on purpose. He followed her toward the next booth, where Lacey and Devin had set up a tiny version of their farm stand. They'd brought a variety of root vegetables, the first of the lettuce and asparagus and buckets of the wildflowers they'd grown in the field at the farm.

"Looks like y'all have had a lot of customers today." Garrett held up a hand to high-five his brother.

"We're about to close up shop, I think. We sold out of Lacey's cookies in the first few hours. Have you seen the weather report lately?" Devin turned his phone around to show Garrett. "Two hours from now, this place is gonna be a swamp. I also heard on the news this morning there was a strong possibility of some flooding along the river north of here."

Garrett frowned. "I knew it had been raining a lot, but I didn't know that."

Someone handed Devin a five and pointed to the flowers. Devin handed over a bouquet. "Thanks, man. Enjoy."

"What's Tanner think? Is he worried?" Tanner was the oldest by seven years. Garrett and Devin both depended on his quiet leadership when it came to the farm.

Devin glanced at Lacey, who was engrossed in conversation with her order pad out, and back to Garrett. "Yeah. He is. We've gotten a lot of rain, but from here to Nashville, they've had nonstop downpours for days. All that water's gotta go somewhere."

"Tanner's worried that the farm will flood?" Abby asked.

Devin shrugged. "It hasn't happened in our lifetime, but yeah, I think he's worried."

Garrett squinted at the heavy clouds, which suddenly seemed a lot more than a little ominous. He put his hand over Abby's on the stroller handle. "Want something to eat?"

"Sure. See you guys."

Before Garrett moved to join her, he leaned in to

speak quietly to Devin. "Keep me posted. I'll be home as soon as I can."

Devin nodded. "You got it."

Garrett caught up with Abby. "How about some shrimp tacos? You ever had them?"

"I've seen them on menus, does that count?"

He rolled his eyes. "Absolutely not. Come with me."

Abby's face was skeptical as he ordered them for her, complete with cabbage slaw and spicy mango salsa, but he saw that expression change when she took her first bite. "Well?"

She made him wait while she finished the first taco and delicately wiped her mouth, before she said, "I still think they're more like a shrimp salad in a tortilla than an actual taco…"

"Oh, come on." He laughed. "Your eyes were rolling back in your head, it was so good."

"You're not wrong." With a chuckle, Abby picked up her second taco and took a bite. Her next words were muffled. "It's so good."

Charlotte started to squirm and fuss in the stroller, so Garrett pulled a bottle out of the bag and set it on the table. He unbuckled the baby, tucked her into position and started to feed her before he noticed Abby's eyes on him. "What?"

"You've come a long way since the first day with Charlotte. Now you barely have to think about it."

He raised his eyebrows. That first day, he'd seriously wondered if he was up for the challenge. "I guess getting thrown into the deep end will do that for you."

She giggled. "You had your shirt buttoned wrong."

He deadpanned her. "It wasn't funny."

She laughed harder. "And your hair was sticking straight up like Albert Einstein."

"It was not." A twitch started at the corner of his mouth because he knew it had been.

"Did you even have socks on with your dress shoes?"

"No," he admitted, and he started to laugh, too. "I couldn't find any. I picked up the first tie I saw on the chair by my bed and draped it around my neck. I have no idea if it matched or not."

"It didn't." She tried to stop, wiping tears from under her eyes, but giggles were still escaping. "I'm sorry. It's funny now thinking back. I bet you were scared out of your mind."

"That's the understatement of the year." Garrett looked down at Charlotte. He may be an unexpected daddy, but he tried to be a good one. He loved her and that had to count for something.

"I think I might have found something that could help you with your search for Charlotte's mom." Abby rubbed a spot of salsa off her cheek with a napkin and pulled her phone out. "I've been reading through Brooklyn's Facebook posts."

"She hasn't posted since she left town." Garrett looked down at the bottle, tipping it so he could see how many ounces were left.

"No, she hasn't. It doesn't look like she's been in contact with her friends either if this post on her page is any indication." Abby tapped on the screen, scrolled for a second and then turned her phone so Garrett could see it.

He leaned forward to read the post she pointed to. "'Girl, answer your phone. Where you been? We need ta party.' Charming."

"Yeah, well, you knew she wasn't hanging out with the best crowd. But when you read further down, like way down, there are some posts about how she wants to go to cosmetology school. I'm wondering if Brooklyn decided to actually do something about it."

"Maybe, but why leave Charlotte? Couldn't she go to cosmetology school here?"

Abby shrugged. "Maybe not if she wanted to steer clear of friends who were trying to get her to party instead."

"That makes the most sense of anything I've heard so far. Unfortunately, we still have to find her. There have to be hundreds of those schools around." Garrett sighed, put the bottle on the table and lifted Charlotte to his shoulder.

"Yeah. I'll keep looking. Maybe there's a clue buried in the comments somewhere."

"Remind me on Monday and I'll take another look at my files. Maybe she said something about her dream place to live in one of my interviews with her. Sometimes I write stuff like that down."

A fat raindrop hit Abby in the forehead. She squinted up at the sky. "I think it's time for us to go."

Garrett nodded. "Yeah, it looks like the bottom's about to fall out."

As they started packing up, the band was doing the same and a few minutes later, Mayor Wynn took the stage.

She cleared her throat. "Hey everyone, as most of you know, I'm Wynn Grant, the mayor here in Red Hill Springs. I'm sorry to say that we're going to close up early this year, for everyone's safety. Thanks so much for coming and y'all be safe going home."

Wynn's brother Joe, the police chief, bounded up the stairs. He said something to Wynn that Abby couldn't hear and then took the mic. "I'm Joe Sheehan, the police chief here in Red Hill Springs. Everyone listen up for an announcement: the bridge over Red Hill Creek is washed out on Highway 43. There are multiple reports of flooding in Triple Creek. If you're headed north, please be careful. Do *not* drive through water that's covering the road, even if you think it isn't deep."

Abby turned to Garrett, eyes dark with concern. "Triple Creek? That's just north of your farm, right?"

His face was serious. "Pretty close. I need to call Tanner."

As Garrett reached for his phone, it buzzed. Around him, he saw his friends reaching for their phones and kissing their wives. He knew what that meant. And it wasn't good.

Garrett checked his message and stood. "I've got to go. I'm on the volunteer fire department and they're calling me in."

Abby didn't hesitate, just held her arms out for the baby. "Take my car. I'll take yours with the car seat and you can pick Charlotte up later."

"Are you sure?"

"Of course." Abby paused in the middle of buckling Charlotte back into the infant seat.

From across the park, he heard someone yell his name and he took a step in that direction. "Be careful, okay? It's going to be dark soon and no one knows how fast the water will rise."

"I'll take care of her, I promise. But Garrett?"

With her keys in his hand, he stopped. "Yeah?"

"Promise me you'll take care of you."

Abby threw a blanket over the stroller and ran for Garrett's SUV—as fast as she could with a crowd of people also hurrying to get out of the park. When she finally made it, she popped the infant seat off the stroller and locked it into place on its base.

"Hey, Abs, got a second?"

Abby peered through the rain and saw Wynn jogging toward her. She thunked the stroller into the back of Garrett's SUV. "If you get in while we talk."

She slammed the rear door shut and slid into the driver's seat, squeezing the rainwater out of her hair. Ugh. The clouds that had been threatening all day hadn't been bluffing.

A second later, Wynn slid into the passenger seat and pushed the hood of her raincoat away from her face.

"Hey, you really know how to throw a party." Abby started the car and pressed the defrost button as the windows started to fog.

"You know it." Wynn groaned, shaking her head. "We'll be trying to regrow the grass for the next four months."

"So, what's up?"

"Tomorrow morning, we'll start sending out teams to check houses. If we need it, the church will open up as a shelter for evacuees from the storm. If that happens, it's going to be all hands on deck. I know you didn't sign up for this, but we'll need you—and Elvis, too."

"Tell me where you need me to go and I'll be there."

If people were in need, she couldn't turn away. She looked out at the dark stew of clouds. "Garrett's out there in this."

"I know." Wynn put her hand over Abby's. "But our volunteer fire department is well trained. And he's been doing this a long time. He'll be okay."

"He also goes to extremes if he thinks he can help."

Wynn smiled. "He does. A lot like someone else I know. I've got to run. Be safe. I'll see you tomorrow."

Abby took a second for a deep breath and a whispered prayer for the first responders' safety. Traffic eased so she put the car in Reverse, slamming the brakes when a knock at the window startled her. She rolled the window down to find Wynn standing there. "What's going on?"

"I just got word there's a child trapped by the flood-waters and the firefighters can't get her to budge. Are you up to getting Elvis and heading out with the next group?"

"Of course, but I have Charlotte."

"I forgot about that." Wynn squeezed her eyes shut, thinking. "Okay, this could work. I'll call Jules and see if she can meet you at your house. You'd have to pick Elvis up, anyway."

"Sounds good."

"Yes? Good. I'll send you more information as I get it." Wynn drew her finger in a circle in the air and behind Abby, flashing blue lights came on. Apparently, Abby was getting a police escort. She sucked in a breath, nerves skittering in her stomach.

It wouldn't be her first trip out with first responders— she'd participated in rescues before—but with unpredictable floodwaters, it would certainly be the most dangerous.

It didn't matter.

There was a little girl out there who was scared and alone with the water rising around her.

Garrett shielded his face against the pelting rain. He and his partner had gotten a call that there was a child stuck on the roof of a mobile home. In rising water like this there were no landmarks, no visible street signs. That they found the mobile home at all was their first break.

That the child was still on the roof? That was a gift from God.

His partner Jackson Andrews steered their small inflatable raft closer to a large oak tree and Garrett tossed a line over one of the larger branches. Anything to give them a little more stability to maintain their position in the fast-moving water.

Another crew was on the other side of the mobile home. At this point, whichever team had the leverage would get the child off the roof.

His boat bumped the side of the mobile home and from a gaping hole in the roof, another small head poked out. There were two?

Jackson apparently realized the same thing because he shouted, "There are two of them!"

The child tried to climb on the roof, wobbled and tumbled backward into the hole. On the other side of the roof, the other child was being helped into a life jacket.

Garrett wasn't sure the roof was going to hold him, but it didn't look like he had much choice. He yelled to Jackson, "Get as close as you can. I'm going over."

In response, Jackson steered the boat closer. He fought against the current to stay as close to the home as possible. Garrett waited for the firefighters on the other side to help the older girl into the boat. Then he took a deep breath and leaped across the water, landing on the roof.

The mobile home rocked with the force of his weight and from inside he heard a weak scream of fear. Unwilling to rock the unsteady trailer any more, he lay down on his stomach and belly crawled over to the jagged opening. Down below, he saw a little boy, around five or six, standing on a kitchen cabinet. Water lapped at the cabinets, at least twelve inches deep and rising.

"I'm Garrett. I'm a firefighter. What's your name?" Garrett looked around the mobile home, checking for any hidden dangers.

"Toby."

"Okay, Toby, I'm gonna get you out of there." The little boy's lips were blue with cold, his skin like marble. Garrett pulled straps off of his utility belt and made a loop that he could drop through the ragged opening. "How old are you, Toby?"

"F-f-five."

"You're a very brave five-year-old." Garrett hung as far into the space as he could without falling in and draped the strap around Toby. The little boy was quick, grabbing on to it with each hand.

"Her is free."

Garrett stopped midmotion. "Your sister is free? The one who got in the boat?"

Toby shook his head vehemently. "No. Her."

He pointed into the bedroom. Garrett couldn't see anything. He grabbed his flashlight and shone it as far into the murky space as he could, eyes roaming over every inch.

With the water still rising, he'd decided to haul Toby out and go back to check, when his flashlight fell on the corner of the dresser. And he could see five tiny fingers with chipped pink polish gripping the edge.

He lifted his head. "We've got another one in here!"

To Toby, he said, "Come on, buddy, let's get you out of there."

In one heaving motion, he swung Toby off the countertop and dragged him onto the roof, so fast that the little boy almost didn't have time to be scared. When his feet grabbed purchase, Toby locked his scrawny little arms around Garrett's neck, burying his face in Garrett's shirt.

Garrett managed to half crawl, half slide to the edge where he unclenched Toby's arms and stuffed them into the life jacket that Jackson tossed him. A few minutes later, with Toby safely curled up on the bottom of the inflatable raft wrapped in a space blanket, Garrett said, "I've got to go back."

"I heard on the radio that they've got another crew on the way. The big sister told Gary and Max that the little one wouldn't come out. She's apparently terrified of men. They asked the sister if the little one could talk and she said no. May have autism. They weren't sure." Jackson managed to keep the boat close, but with the water rising, the current was getting stronger.

At least the rain had slacked off. For now.

"That complicates things a little bit." Garrett started back across the roof as the whine of another motor sounded across the water. He glanced up, looked away and then back again. Was that... No. It couldn't be...

"Abby?"

Chapter Ten

As their very small boat zipped across the water toward a red dot on a GPS screen, Abby kept a firm grip on Elvis's collar and a constant stream of silent prayers going up.

More information had been trickling out from the firefighters who'd rescued the trapped child's sister. According to her driver, a firefighter named Jed, the little girl's name was Maya—three years old, nonverbal and terrified of men.

Abby hoped she liked dogs.

The light was dimming, daylight fading. They weren't going to have long.

She heard the motor throttle back and looked up. The mobile home was directly in front of them, tilted at an angle, like it had been pushed off its blocks by the rushing water. One of the volunteer firefighters lay on his belly near a gash in the roof.

Jed dropped the motor speed even more, easing up to the side of the mobile home at idle speed. And now that they were closer, she realized the water was over the steps by at least a few feet, maybe more. There was no way that Elvis would be able to get in there. But she could.

"Abby?"

Her head jerked up as she heard her name. Garrett was the firefighter on the roof of the trailer. His face was blank with shock. "What are you doing here?"

"I'm here to help." The rain had slacked to a sprinkle, but dark clouds billowed in the west. They weren't going to have long between the sun going down and the next round of storms. To Jed, she said, "If you can pull up next to the roof and cut power, I'll be ready to go."

Abby crouched in the boat, keeping her center of gravity low, until they were just close enough. Standing now, Garrett gripped her hand and swung her onto the roof. The whole thing careened under them, shifting with her added weight. She dropped down, mimicking Garrett's position, and army crawled closer.

"Abby, how—where's Charlotte?"

"Jules is watching her. Wynn asked me to come since the little girl likely has autism. I have search-and-rescue experience. Not a ton, but this isn't my first time coaxing someone out of debris. Is this gonna be a problem for you?"

He looked directly into her eyes. "Not at all. She's in the bedroom, on top of a chest of drawers against the wall."

"Does she look injured?"

He gave a slight shake of the head. "Not that I can tell, but every time I try to get a better look, she starts screaming."

Abby followed the beam of light from his flashlight

down into the mobile home. It was dark in there. The water was murky and brown, lapping at the edges of the countertops in the kitchen. And at the very farthest reach of the flashlight, she could see the little girl's white-knuckle grip on the edge of the chest of drawers. *Oh, sweet girl.*

With one last quick prayer for the right words, Abby shimmied closer. "Maya? My name's Abby. If you can hear me, can you wiggle your fingers?"

For a moment, there was no response, then a hair of a second when the grip loosened and the fingers moved.

"Good job! That's really good. We're here to help you stay safe in the water. Can you peek your head around so I can see your pretty eyes?"

Again the seconds ticked by.

"We can't wait much longer, Abby. It's getting dark." Garrett swung his feet around and got one booted leg through the opening before the little girl started screaming. Terrified, hysterical screams.

"Stop! Garrett, stop." Abby drew in a slow, patient breath. They were all stressed. It was fine. She said quietly, "You trust me with Charlotte. Trust me now. Give me a few minutes to work and if I can't get her out safely, then we'll do what we have to, okay?"

She held her hand out for the flashlight and, with his eyes on hers, he placed it in her hand. "How much daylight do we have?"

"Ten minutes, maybe fifteen. Then it gets too dangerous for anyone to be out in this mess."

"Got it." She leaned forward so Maya could hear her voice. "Hey, Maya, he's gone. It's just me. Can I see your sweet face now?"

The seconds ticked by, turning into a minute and Abby wondered if Maya was too scared to cooperate or maybe she just didn't understand. But then, a curly mop of blond curls appeared along with a set of big blue eyes. "There you are! Can you see me, too?"

Maya nodded, the curls bouncing on her head. Abby smiled. "Good. I need to ask you a couple of questions."

Another nod.

"Can you swim?"

A negative shake of the head.

"Yes?" Garrett asked.

"No." Abby locked her gaze on his, stifling a scream as the mobile home shifted. Garrett grabbed her arm as she started to slide and hauled her back to the edge of the opening in the roof.

"We can't wait any longer, which means I'm gonna have to go in after her."

For a second, she thought he would argue, but instead, he gave her a firm nod. "We do this together. I've got your back. Whatever you need."

"Thanks, Garrett." Abby leaned forward. "Maya?"

The little girl peered around the corner again.

"Do you like dogs?"

A single nod in answer.

"Me too! My dog is in the boat out here. I bet he'd like to meet you. Would you like that?"

Another single nod.

"I'm coming down. There'll be a big splash and a second later, I'll be right there beside you, okay?"

Before she could rethink her decision, Abby dropped through the opening in the roof into the kitchen of the mobile home. One foot landed on the floor, the other on something unseen in the water, her ankle twisting underneath her. She sucked in a breath.

Garrett's voice came from above. "Abby?"

"It's okay. I'm okay." She held her breath and counted. *One, two, three, four.* Eased out the breath as the pain started to lessen. "I'm good. I'm going to the bedroom."

With the flashlight shining in front of her, she could see Maya squatting on top of the chest of drawers, dressed in only an oversized T-shirt. The tiny lips were purple, the little girl's whole body trembling. Abby smiled. "Well, hello there. You must be Maya. Very nice to meet you."

That silly bit of politeness elicited a scant smile.

"You ready to get out of here?"

A vehement shake of the head.

"No?"

Maya pointed across the room.

"Is there something you need from over there?"

More nodding. Abby fought the desire to grab the little girl and sprint out of that murky, disgusting water as fast as she could. But a few seconds spent here could save them a lot more in the long run. She sludged a few steps further into the bedroom and heard Garrett's warning tone. "Abby…"

Maya let out a keening cry.

"It's okay, Maya." She started humming "Jesus Loves Me" while shining the flashlight around the room. Finally, she caught sight of a stuffed dog wedged between the headboard and the wall. Maybe? She plucked it out. "Is this little guy what you were looking for?"

Maya reached with one hand for the stuffed dog

and Abby edged closer. "You think you can come and get him?"

Abby opened her arms and Maya jumped into them, scrambling up Abby's body to get as far away from the water as she could. Keeping her voice as calm and steady as she could, Abby said, "Good girl, Maya. You're doing so good."

In the kitchen, she glanced up at the space above, where she'd dropped in. If she had to get out that way, she could, but it would be difficult, but maybe… She sloshed a few more feet through water nearly up to her waist and tugged on the door. It cracked a couple of inches.

She called upward. "Garrett, can you get Jed to pull up close to the door? I think I can get it open."

Garrett relayed her message and she heard the boat's motor pick up. It was hard to get enough leverage while holding Maya, but she put one foot on the frame and tugged as hard as she could on the doorknob. "I can't get it to budge. It's stuck on something."

A split second later, she heard a splash outside and Garrett wrenched the door open. One more obstacle down.

Now to get Maya on the boat. "Elvis, watch me. Look, Maya. There's my dog. He's waiting for you to come and give him a big hug, just like you do with your little dog. Do you think you can do that? I know you can. You've been so brave."

With all her strength, Abby lifted Maya onto the edge of the boat, ignoring the sudden tearing pain in her side. Through gritted teeth, she said, "Elvis, give hugs."

Elvis leaned forward, resting his nose on Maya's

shoulder. The terrified little girl wrapped her arms around him and buried her face in his soft fur.

Abby breathed a sigh of relief. The hardest part was over, and now that they were out, the fire rescue team worked quickly—and quietly, obviously trying not to scare Maya more.

"They have an ambulance waiting just outside the flooded area to take the two of you to the hospital to meet her siblings." Garrett touched her arm. "You were amazing, Abby."

"We make a good team. Thanks for the muscle."

He grinned. "Anytime."

Above them, the ruined trailer groaned and shifted. Garrett shouted. Jed reached a hand out and heaved Abby into the boat. She was dripping, soaked to the skin, shivering and exhausted. But they had all three kids safely out of that mobile home and on their way to being reunited.

She sat next to Maya against the side of the boat. The little girl kept her face hidden, but she scooched closer, bringing Elvis with her. Abby put her arm around them both, sucking in a breath as she pressed on her side with the other one.

"We'll have y'all on dry land just as fast as we can. Hang on." Jed turned the boat away from the ruined trailer and toward safety.

An hour and a half later, Garrett strode through the glass door leading into the ER. He'd only stopped long enough to shower off the mud and get into dry clothes. After a quick call to Jules to make sure Charlotte was still okay, he'd come straight to the hospital.

Almost everyone had gotten out in time, loading their cars with their belongings and driving out, but in total, he and his team had rescued one elderly couple and two families—including the children in the mobile home and one couple with a day-old baby—who'd been trapped by the rising water.

A handful of dogs, a couple of cats and a parrot named Bert had also been boated out by various first responders and taken to the local vet for boarding until their owners were safely able to return home.

Garrett heard from the paramedics that Abby was in the ER and he couldn't rest until he knew she was okay. He found her in one of the small rooms, scrolling through her phone. It looked like she'd managed a shower too, because her hair was damp and she was wearing an oversized green hospital gown.

He cleared his throat. "They'll just give anyone an exam room these days."

"Ha ha, very funny." Abby smirked up at him and the coil of tension he'd been carrying since she sped away on the boat unwound just a bit.

But she had an IV hooked into her arm and when he stepped closer, she pulled the blanket up self-consciously.

"What's going on here? Did something happen that I don't know about?"

Her cheeks colored. "It seems that I reopened a wound when I was 'traipsing around in the flood,' as the ER doctor put it."

He dragged a chair up to the side of the bed and sat. "Are you okay?"

"I'm fine. Nothing a few more stitches and a whopping dose of antibiotics won't fix. Apparently flood-water really is as disgusting as it looks." She rolled her eyes. "Please stop making that face. I'm going to be fine. How's Charlotte?"

"Apparently, she's loving life with the Quinns. Jules said she is fascinated by all the kids and the older ones are fighting over who gets to hold her, so she is in hog heaven."

"I'm sure." Abby laughed. "Did you get in touch with Tanner and Devin?"

"Yep. Talked to Tanner just now. They're dry at the moment. The flooding is supposed to crest tomorrow afternoon and then start receding. We're at a higher elevation than the neighborhoods that flooded today, but tomorrow morning we're going to move as many of the livestock as we can to higher ground."

"It's never flooded before?"

"We've had high water in the swampy areas, but the water never reached the fields and pastures, much less the house. This time? The amount of rain dumped upstream... I think the weather people on the news are calling it *unprecedented*. We won't know if we're out of the woods until tomorrow night."

"You can use the barn at my house if you need it."

"That's a good idea. I'll let Tanner and Devin know."

"Good. And I'll keep the babies tomorrow so you can help move everyone to high ground."

"Okay. That sounds like a plan." Garrett reached for her hand, gently sliding it into his. "I was so worried when I saw you coming in on that boat. But I didn't need to be. You're a pro, Abby."

"I appreciate that. Both the concern and the compliment." Then, "Have you heard anything more about the kids?"

"They were reunited with each other here at the hospital. They got checked out by a doctor and they got away with minor cuts and bruises. The oldest—who is ten—said her mom was at work, but she couldn't remember where." He rubbed her fingers gently with his thumb.

"What will happen to them?"

"My guess is they'll go to an emergency foster home until Monday, so a caseworker can do a little digging. It's not ideal, but they're safe and together. It's something."

"You're right. It's a lot, actually."

Her eyes had dark smudges underneath them. When she yawned, he wondered if he needed to leave so she could rest. "Do you want me to let you sleep?"

"No. I tried. I just keep replaying the rescue over and over again in my mind." The admission slipped out, revealing that this afternoon's adventure hadn't been the walk in the park for her that she wanted him to believe.

"How about this? Scoot over." He slipped out of his shoes, nudged her over and climbed into the bed beside her, snugging her into the curve of his arm. "I've been saving these videos for when I had time to watch them. It's Abbott and Costello. Have you seen them?"

"Not that I know of."

Garrett tsked. "Your education is sorely lacking. You're going to love them."

Holding his phone where she could see it, he started the *Who's on First* episode. Within two minutes, she was giggling, and by four minutes in, she was wiping tears from under her eyes. He'd seen this episode at least twenty times, but seeing it through Abby's eyes made it even better.

He was content. Today had been incredibly stressful and he was tired, but he needed this. Holding her, laughing with her—there was nowhere else he'd rather be.

Somewhere in the back of his mind that thought set off alarm bells, but he shut them off without a thought.

Chapter Eleven

Abby blew hair off her forehead and looked around at her living room. It was completely trashed. There were bouncy seats and toys, burp cloths and baby bottles littering the floor from one end to the other.

Next time there was a flood, she was not going to volunteer to keep all the Triple Creek Ranch babies. Moving cows and angry pigs had to be easier than this. She had baby cereal stuck to her hair and spit-up on her shirt, three cribs lined up in the guest room and a newborn goat in the bathroom.

Two of the babies were asleep. The third one, Eli, she could see on the video monitor with his thumb in his mouth. He was "singing" himself to sleep. Jules's youngest was in the playpen in the living room, playing with some toys.

Jules dropped into a chair. "I'm not even kidding when I say if someone offered me a free spa day, I would tell them I'm too tired."

"I think you're delirious." Abby picked up her mug of tea, which she'd just warmed in the microwave for the fourth time, and limped over to her chair. She just wanted to sit down for five minutes. Every muscle in her body ached after her adventures fighting the flood yesterday.

The watch on her wrist buzzed and she thought she might cry. It was time to feed Garrett's baby goat who, as the runt of the litter of triplets, was improbably named Hercules and was currently in her guest bathroom because he couldn't keep his body temp up.

Any other time, she'd be thrilled to feed a baby goat. He was the size of a toy poodle and adorable. But her feet were so tired, she couldn't feel them anymore. Three infants plus goat were no joke.

Not to mention, the antibiotics she was on after her dip into the floodwaters were making her sick to her stomach. Super fun.

"Time to feed the goat." She hauled herself to her feet. The other two newborn kids were in one stall in the barn with their mother. The rest of the goats were in stall number two. Lacey and Garrett were on their way with a couple of horses to stay in stalls number three and four. The rest of the animals had either been moved to pasture on higher ground or were staying with other people.

The rattle of a horse trailer on the gravel driveway alerted her to Garrett's arrival. She peeked out the window as he parked in the lit area of the yard and slid out of the farm truck. In his cowboy hat and jeans, Garrett fully looked the part of a rancher today.

Jules stopped at the window beside her and hummed appreciatively. "I love a good cowboy hat."

Abby laughed. "Get out of here and back to your children. It looks like reinforcements have arrived."

"If you're sure, I'll grab Micah and head home. The other kids are going to be hungry and as good as my oldest is with the kids, he is a terrible cook." Jules slung a diaper bag over her shoulder and reached into the play area for Micah, stopping on her way to the door to give Abby a hug. "I'm so glad you're here. Thanks for letting me hang out with you today."

"I couldn't have managed without you." Abby heard a thin bleat from the bathroom. "And I better get in there before he wakes up the human babies. See you tomorrow."

When Abby opened the door to the bathroom, Hercules bounded out. She scooped him up into her arms. He was black and white and fluffy and nuzzled her face with his nose. "Poor Hercules, you have no idea where you are, do you?"

As she talked, his little tail was going ninety miles an hour. He was pretty new in general, so bottle feeding wasn't second nature for him yet. She eased down onto the floor of the bathroom and pulled a towel over her lap. With the fingers of one hand, she opened his mouth and when she stuck the bottle in, he grabbed hold. "That's the way, bud. You got it. Oh, you're hungry, aren't you?"

He stopped for a little breather, bumping her face with his forehead.

She laughed and repositioned the bottle for him. "It's over here."

By the time she finished giving him the bottle, nearly nodding off herself, she was pretty convinced that she had as much milk on her as he had in his tummy. He was calm and sleepy, so she took a moment to enjoy a little snuggle before tucking him into his box.

Finally. All the babies were in bed.

She reached up for the counter to haul herself off the floor and nearly screamed as she grabbed a firm hand instead.

Garrett grinned as he pulled her to her feet. "I'm impressed. All the kids are fed and asleep and I met the pizza delivery guy outside which makes me *so* incredibly happy. Lacey's already stuffing her face."

"I heard that, Garrett." Lacey appeared in the door to the hall with a piece of supreme pizza in her hand. Her dark hair was in a messy bun on top of her head and she had a streak of mud on her cheek. "Also, it's true. It's the best thing I've ever eaten in my entire life."

Garrett leaned over and scratched the goat's tiny head. "Hercules seems to be holding his own. Tomorrow we'll put him in with the others so he can learn to be a goat. How are you holding up?"

"No problems." She wavered on her feet, contradicting her own statement. "Yeah, wow, I'm tired."

"Come get some pizza. I'm feeling better by the minute." Lacey waved Abby into the kitchen. "You've had a busy day. The twins are a handful by themselves. No wonder you're tired."

"Sit." Garrett shoved Abby into a chair at the kitchen table as she protested.

"You guys have been working all day, too. And I had help. Tell me what's going on now." Despite her protest, she took a bite of the pepperoni pizza Garrett put in front of her. A few seconds later, he set a fizzing cola by the plate.

"We sandbagged a couple of areas that we thought might flood." Lacey took another bite of pizza. "Garrett, Devin and Tanner moved most of the animals, except for the two we just put in the barn. We were working them pretty hard. The other horses are in the pasture at Red Hill Farm. Jordan's going to board them with her horses."

"The cows are on high ground. The pigs are with Mr. Haney on his farm, but let me tell you, those pigs were not happy." Garrett finished his first piece of pizza and refilled his cup from a can of soda. "The animals will be safe. We may have some work—a lot of work—to do to rebuild the lower pasture areas, but I don't think the water's going to get up to the house or barn."

"Hey, guys." Devin opened the back door and stood in the opening while he toed off his muddy boots. "Is that pizza? I'm starving."

Abby frowned. "Where's Tanner?"

"Staying at the house. He won't leave. We didn't even try to argue." Garrett reached for another piece.

"Garrett, what about the kittens?"

"No worries. We put them inside in one of the upstairs bathrooms. They'll be safely out of harm's way." He cut his eyes at her. "Unless you want me to bring them over here?"

"Uh, no. We have enough babies in this house, thank you very much. Tanner can take care of the kittens."

"Tanner might want to run away by the time the mama cat stops her caterwauling." Devin grinned. "Get it, *cat*erwauling?"

"Ugh. That was terrible." Garrett shook his head. "I'm just thankful the puppy incident is behind us."

"The puppy incident?" Abby asked with a mouthful of pizza.

"You haven't heard about that?" With a piece of pizza in one hand, his soda in the other and a wide grin on his face, Devin sat back. "Someone left a litter of barely weaned, starving puppies in the alleyway behind the main street shops. Garrett the Noble took them home and fed them every couple of hours for two weeks. He hauled those puppies everywhere, trying to fatten them up."

"Oh my goodness, the poor little things. Did they make it?" Abby's face was stricken.

Garrett laughed and put his arm around her shoulders, the unconscious gesture making her feel like she was a part of their group. "They're fine."

Devin scoffed. "Of course they made it. Those were the fattest puppies you've ever seen."

"Hang on, I've got a pic." Lacey was flipping through her phone. "Here it is."

Garrett was seated on the ground with nine pudgy black and white puppies crawling all over him. His head was thrown back in a laugh.

"They're precious. What happened to them?"

Lacey rolled her eyes. "We begged and pleaded and called in all the favors from everyone we knew until finally they were all adopted."

"You saved their little lives, Garrett."

He slung his arm around her chair and thumped his chest with his fist. "Yep. Heart of gold."

Puppies. Baby. Special stroller for a little boy who

needed one. Not to mention how he looked in jeans and a cowboy hat. Was it any wonder she was head over heels for him?

Wait—*was* she falling for him?

That didn't seem like something she would do.

But Garrett wasn't like anyone else she'd ever met. Oh, boy, she had a feeling that, floodwaters or no floodwaters, she was about to be in over her head.

Heart of gold? Garrett wasn't even sure where that came from except that it sounded ridiculous. He was definitely more tired than he thought he was.

"Hang on." Devin raised a cynical eyebrow. "You haven't heard the best part, Abby. Word got around about what Garrett did for the puppies and people started dropping all kinds of animals off at the end of our lane. Kittens and puppies galore. One person even tied a donkey to the fence and drove off."

"What? That's not cool."

Garrett finished off his pizza and brushed the crumbs off his fingers. "Well, he is a pretty great donkey."

"He is, that's true. We named him Sheriff and put him in the field with the cows. And now he's a watchdog. Watch-donkey?" Lacey laughed. "I have no idea. But I know I'm exhausted and this is pathetic, but the babies will be up in a couple of hours for a bottle and I've got to take a shower and get at least a few hours' sleep before we're back at it tomorrow."

"Good idea." Devin picked up the paper plates on the table, reached for his cane with the other hand and limped to the trash can. "I'm going to my Narcotics Anonymous meeting and then I'll be back to hit the sack myself. I have a feeling we're going to have more long days in the future before things get back to normal at the ranch."

"Yeah, we all need to hit the hay early." Garrett gathered up the pizza boxes and drink cups that were scattered on the table. "I'll be right back."

Garrett walked outside and dumped the trash in the big trash can. When he turned around, he was facing the pasture behind Abby's rental house. The grass glowed with a blue-green hue and the moon coming up on the horizon was spectacular. The storms had passed and he could see every star in the Milky Way. He stuck his head in the back door. "Hey, Abs, come here for a minute."

She joined him at the porch rail and, as if it were the most natural thing in the world, his arm slid around her back. "Look at that moon."

With a sigh, she gazed at the huge golden orb slowly rising from the horizon. "It's incredible."

Maybe it was silly and a huge mistake to pull her closer. After all, he didn't know what the next few months would bring for her…or him, for that matter. What he did know was that he felt good when he was with her. With other people, he often felt that he had to always be on. Always meet the expectations of other people. With Abby, he just felt…accepted. And after watching her with that little girl yesterday, he thought the ability to convey caring without judgment might just be her superpower.

He looked down at her. "We couldn't have made it through these last couple of days without you. I couldn't have made it through last month without you."

"This may seem a little out-there, but I feel like God

put me in just the right place at the right time. I'm just glad I could help."

"It's not out-there at all. I feel that way, too." He tilted her chin up and kissed her gently, just a soft brush of his lips against hers before he turned back to the moon.

"I'm…not sure where we're going with this, Garrett." Her eyes stayed on the moon, but the question was in her voice.

"I have a habit of bouncing from one thing to another as the spirit moves me. I enjoy my life. Even when I'm suddenly making gruel for nine scrawny puppies at all hours of the night. It's the adventure of it all, I guess." He looked down into her eyes, which looked huge and dark in the shadows of her back porch. "But I like where I am, right at this exact moment."

"Me, too." Her watch buzzed. She stopped the alarm and looked up. "Time to feed Hercules."

"I'll feed him. You get some sleep."

"I *am* tired," she admitted.

The back door opened and a bleary-eyed Lacey stood there in her pajamas and robe, damp hair curling down her back, Charlotte in her arms. "Your baby's hungry, Garrett."

Abby smiled, her face softening as she reached for Charlotte. "I'll get the baby, you get the goat?"

"Sounds like a bad country song." He hummed a few bars as he followed her into the house to fix the bottles, her laughter wrapping around him.

And he smiled because despite all the crazy stuff going on, this at least was right.

Three days after the night spent waiting out the flood at Abby's house, Garrett turned Reggie toward the barn, keeping pace with Devin, who was up on Icarus. Reggie was Devin's horse, but the unvarnished truth was that if Garrett was going to help with the livestock, he needed Reggie. The horse had the talent. Garrett was just along for the ride.

The pond had turned into a lake and the back fields were either underwater or too muddy to use. It was a mess, but the house and barn had survived. They'd survive, too, but it was going to set them back at a time when they were just getting on their feet.

He sighed.

Devin glanced over at him as they kept the horses to a slow walk. "How's Charlotte doing in day care?"

"Oh, *she's* doing fine. I, on the other hand, am a wreck after I drop her off." In all the hubbub, Garrett had almost forgotten that six weeks was the magic age and, if he forfeited Charlotte's spot, she'd be on the waiting list at least another month, maybe more. So, with no other alternative, she'd started on Monday and he'd had a lump in his throat all the way to the office. "Abby asked if she could pick her up a little bit early and bring her home for me."

Devin rolled his eyes toward the finally blue sky. "You two are pitiful."

Garrett made a derisive snort. "As if you're not wrapped around the itty-bitty fingers of your twins."

"No doubt." Devin shook his head. "I never dreamed I'd settle down and be a family man, especially here. But I love it. Wouldn't change a thing."

Garrett knew his brother deserved the contentment he was feeling now. Devin had run from their past for a long time. But Garrett would be lying if he didn't admit, at least to himself, that he envied his brother that domestic bliss.

He rode in silence for a few beats, then perked up as he remembered his favorite moment of the day. "Hey, did you see me and Reggie catch that calf this afternoon? It was epic."

Devin laughed. "Yeah, I saw it, but you're gonna feel it. It's been a long time since Mom packed us a lunch and we rode horses all day every day. You're gonna be sore tomorrow."

"Tomorrow?" Garrett snorted. "I'm gonna need help to get into the house today."

As the horses approached the barn, he saw Abby step out the door in her sock feet with Charlotte in her arms. Her cheerful yellow rain boots were covered in mud and sitting by the mat.

He'd barely seen Abby since the night they'd stayed at her house. They'd crossed paths in the office, but she was busy seeing clients and he, for the most part, had been working from dawn to dusk with his brothers to salvage what they could of the rain-soaked crops in the low areas of their farm.

Garrett guided Reggie closer to the house so he could speak to her. "Hello, ladies."

"Hi. You guys are looking good on horseback. Thanks for letting me pick Charlotte up. I missed her. Hey, Devin," she said.

"Abby." Devin tipped his hat at her and she grinned. Garrett rolled his eyes. His brother, the former rodeo heartthrob.

Abby laughed. "Looks like y'all have had a busy day."

"It's been an interesting week, to say the least. Garrett, I'm gonna get Icarus put away."

As Devin turned away, Reggie pranced sideways toward the barn, wanting to follow, but the big horse was much too much of a gentleman to really press the point. Garrett patted his neck and he settled down. "How was your day?"

"Long." She shrugged a little. "Word's gotten out that I'm seeing people and I'm getting referrals right and left."

"You need anything?"

A small head shake. "I'll be fine after a good night's sleep. No worries."

"Staying for dinner?" Reggie's ear flicked back and Garrett would've sworn he'd heard the word *dinner*.

"I'm not sure. I'm exhausted. I just needed some Charlotte snuggles for a few minutes." Her hair wafted in the breeze as she looked down at Charlotte. The last of the afternoon sunlight speared through the trees, bathing her and the baby in rose gold.

Garrett blinked.

"I'm going to head home soon."

Reggie was restless, dancing in place. Garrett took him in a tight circle and stopped him again in front of Abby. "If you can keep Charlotte a little while longer, I'll get Reggie settled and then I'll be on dad time."

"Of course."

He wanted to slide off and walk Reggie into the barn, but he wasn't sure his legs would hold him, which would be humiliating. So, he waited until he was in the barn and Devin could hold Reggie's head before he tried to get off. He managed to do it without whimpering, so that was something.

"You good?"

Garrett let his head drop against the saddle. "Oh, yeah. Good."

"Your voice is, like, two octaves higher than usual. You need to borrow my cane?"

"Maybe." Garrett laughed. "What I need to do is ride more often. This is embarrassing."

"You can ride anytime." Devin took Reggie's bridle off and gave him a good scratch. "At some point, you're gonna ask Abby out, like on a real date, right? It's getting a little embarrassing, the way you guys look at each other when you think no one is watching."

Garrett unbuckled the girth and lifted the saddle off of Reggie's back, suppressing the groan as his legs protested the movement. He called back to Devin from the tack room. "When exactly am I going to have time to take Abby on a date?"

"How about tomorrow?" Devin hung up the bridle and picked up Reggie's soft halter before sliding it into place.

"It wouldn't be much of a date with Charlotte along. Not complaining, just being realistic. Plus, I think Abby's got something at the elementary school tomorrow."

"Friday, then. Tanner will keep Charlotte."

"Tanner will *what*?" Their oldest brother walked into the barn and hung the keys to the ATV on a nail by the door.

"Babysit Charlotte so Garrett can go on a real date." Devin led Reggie into the stall where his hay was waiting for him. Garrett picked up a brush and started working the mud out of Reggie's coat while Devin cleaned his hooves. They'd been ingrained from an early age to take care of their animals' needs before they took care of their own. Neither of them really even considered doing anything else.

Garrett paused in the brushing and gave Devin a pointed look. "You don't have to do that, Tanner. I can find a babysitter *if* I need one."

Tanner leaned on the doorjamb, lifted his ball cap and rubbed his head before settling the cap back into place. "I can knock off early Friday and keep her. Late afternoon work for you?"

Garrett paused. "Ah, yeah. I guess? I think. I mean, I haven't asked Abby yet. You think I should?"

"Yes!" his brothers said in unison.

"Okay, okay. I guess it's unanimous then."

Devin lifted his fist up for a bump. "Dude. I'm proud of you. Now go ask her before you lose your nerve."

"I'm not gonna lose my—" Garrett stopped. What was he thinking? Devin was offering to finish grooming Reggie. He held out the brush. "Okay, thanks."

In his mind, he jogged toward the house with a plan to ask Abby out on a date. In reality, he moved at a snail's pace, clenching his jaw to keep from groaning out loud because his muscles were screaming at him.

But Devin was right. Abby wasn't just another girl to date. She was special and he had to make a move or she was going to slip away, back to her old life, and she would just be someone he knew once.

Chapter Twelve

Abby dumped the cutting board of chopped bell pepper pieces into the pot of chili and reached for an onion, stopping midmotion as she caught the look on Lacey's face. "What? I never said I knew how to cook."

Lacey laughed and held up her hands. "I'm just joking. No judgment here. My dad was our cook after my mom left us. He was terrible. It was pure self-preservation that I learned to cook."

"Do you see your mom now?" Abby kept her eyes carefully on the onion she was cutting.

"Never. Not even sure she's alive, to be honest. You?"

"No. She calls every once in a while, just often enough to pretend she cares. My dad died when I was a baby in a military training accident."

"I'm sorry. It's tough losing a parent."

"I guess. I wish I'd gotten to know him, but it's hard to miss something you never had, you know?"

Lacey looked skeptical, but didn't say anything. Instead, she asked, "So your dad died when you were a baby. Where did you and your mom live?"

The onions were stinging her eyes and Abby blinked. "I didn't live with my mom. After our house was destroyed by a tornado when I was five, I went to live with my grandma. She was the best. She'd wrap you in big hugs and she always smelled like rose-scented lotion."

Her grandma had passed away when she was nine, leaving the house to Abby's aunt, who'd grudgingly allowed her to stay with them. She still kept in touch with her cousins from time to time, but it wasn't like having a real family. "I don't have family. Not like this, anyway."

"So are you and Garrett gonna make this a thing or what?"

Abby went still. "Uh…"

Her eyes on the pot of chili she'd gone back to stirring, Lacey said, "All I'm saying is that you should think about it. He's sweet and funny and he really cares about everything."

Thinking carefully, Abby replied, "I like Garrett. I like Red Hill Springs. I love Charlotte. I enjoy being with you guys."

"That's not exactly what I asked." Laccy tasted the chili and added some more cumin to the pot, before turning to Abby with her hand on her hip. "So?"

"Does he know you're talking to me about him?"

"Oh, no. No, no, no." Lacey laughed. "He would die."

Abby rested a hand on her forehead, her eyes on Lacey's. "I went on some dates in college, but I've never had a boyfriend. I don't even have family memories to fall back on. I don't think I'm a very good risk in the love department."

"Oh, honey. Have you met me and Devin? All that stuff is great, but if you don't have it, that's what counseling is for. All I'm saying is, maybe you should go for it." Lacey laughed again. "It's hard. Relationships are hard. Not saying it's not. It's a lot of work, but it's also really worth it."

"I hear you, wise one."

Lacey giggled. "You're the best, you know that? I've loved having you around this last month. It makes me think about what it would be like to have a sister. I've always wanted one."

"Me, too." Emotion—which she usually had so tightly under control—clogged her throat. She hardly ever cried. She prayed instead, giving her tears to the Lord. But at Lacey's words, her eyes filled, threatening to spill over.

Lacey glanced at her face. "Oh my goodness, you have to stop or I'll start crying, too, and we can't have tears in the chili."

From the living room, Abby heard Garrett come in the door. She grabbed Lacey's arm. "Not. Another. Word. I'm serious."

Lacey made a locking motion with her fingers over her lips.

Garrett stuck his head in the kitchen. "Hey Abs, can I talk to you for a minute?"

She followed him into the living room. "Is everything okay?"

He looked at the floor. "Tanner offered to babysit Charlotte Friday night. I was thinking, if you're free, that we might go out, like on a real date. What do you say?"

Butterflies multiplied in her stomach and she forced herself to focus on his handsome, earnest face. He seemed confident, but when he looked up, his eyes gave him away. He was nervous, just like she was.

She thought about the ridiculous conversation with Lacey. Despite the absurdity, maybe Lacey was right. She and Garrett had taken care of Charlotte together. They'd played "house," acted like they were parents.

They'd shared kisses.

And now, he was offering her the chance to see if there was actually something there, something real, not just circumstance.

He cleared his throat. "So, Abby Scott...do you want to go on a date with me?"

She smiled. "Yes. I'd love to go on a date with you."

His face lit up and he wrapped his arms around her, picking her up in a hug, setting her down instantly as he yelped in pain.

"Garrett? What's wrong?"

Waving away her concern, he eased down into Tanner's recliner. "I'm—ah—not used to being in the saddle all day."

She tried not to laugh, covering her mouth with her hand, but his face was so crestfallen, she couldn't help it. A delicate little snort came out.

His head snapped up and he narrowed his eyes. She laughed harder.

"I'm glad my predicament is amusing to you. Hopefully I'll be able to walk tomorrow so we can go on that date."

"I'm sure you'll be fine." She picked up her keys and called into the kitchen. "I'm heading out, Lacey. And Garrett needs some ibuprofen."

His laugh followed her out the door.

Later, curled up in front of the fire with Elvis by her side, she hoped she'd done the right thing in saying yes to Garrett. Going on a date with him, that wasn't scary. He was fun to be with and she was looking forward to it.

It was the rest of it that scared her. The possibilities. She'd been hurt by people who were supposed to love her—her mom, her aunt. Trusted the wrong people. She wanted to believe that, this time, she could trust that her heart would be safe in someone else's hands, but it was a big leap of faith.

She wasn't sure she was ready.

Her phone buzzed and the sight of her boss's name again sent a jolt of adrenaline through her system. She had a choice. She could go back to her life, go back to traveling and protect her heart from a possible heartache. Or she could take a chance with Garrett, risk it all.

And maybe lose it all, too.

She just hoped she was making the right choice.

Garrett swung through the doors into the law office he shared with Wynn Grant, a tray of coffees in his hand and a bag of doughnuts under his arm. Which on second thought might not be the best idea, since they were likely smushed beyond recognition, but he didn't care.

He whistled a happy melody as he dramatically placed one of the cups of coffee on Bess's desk. His assistant was on the phone and looked up with one suspicious eyebrow raised. The second cup went to Wynn as he switched from whistling to singing.

She laughed. "What is up with you today?"

He did a spin, one of his signature dance moves, remembered his sore legs, and flopped down in one of the office chairs. "You are looking at a man *with a date*."

Wynn's eyes widened over the top of the takeout cup. "Oh, really? With who?"

"None other than the beautiful, mysterious Abby."

"She's not mysterious. She's just…Abby. But wow."

"Exactly. Wow. I don't know why I didn't think of it before." He opened the bag, pulled out a smashed doughnut and took a bite.

"Are those doughnuts? Give me one."

He tossed the bag onto her desk. "I'm going to take her somewhere nice for dinner. Somewhere with no kids menu."

Wynn raised one amused eyebrow. "I see the appeal. So what made you take this momentous step?"

"My brothers threatened me."

She snorted and took a pink frosted doughnut with sprinkles out of the bakery bag.

"I'm joking. They *encouraged* me to ask her out. Tanner's watching the baby." He picked up his coffee and took a sip.

"Wow, he really must want you out of his hair. But all kidding aside, that's a pretty big step for Tanner."

"Yeah. It was Devin's suggestion. I guess he's decided that Tanner needs to rejoin the land of the living. It's been fifteen years, almost."

"I can't imagine that kind of grief just goes away."

Garrett looked down at his cup. "I don't think it does. I think about them every day and they weren't mine, not like they were his."

"That's understandable." She sat back in her chair,

her coffee cup in her hand. "So, you're taking my friend out on a date. I have so many questions."

He grinned. "Stop. You're way too quick for your own good."

"She needs some fun in her life. I'm just glad she decided to turn down her boss's request for her to go back to work. It'll be good for her to stick around for a while."

"Her what?" Garrett suddenly didn't feel like whistling anymore. Instead, he felt a knot in the pit of his stomach.

Wynn closed her mouth sharply and he could almost see her mind turning, trying to figure out how to spin what she'd just said.

He sighed. "No, she didn't tell me. And yes, you should feel bad."

She blinked a few more times, clearly scrambling for words, which was very unlike his partner. "Look. I'm sure if it had been important to her she would've mentioned it to you."

"She told you," he pointed out.

"Yes, but only because I forced her to. She's working here in Red Hill Springs for a reason. I'm sure she didn't tell you about her boss's offer because she wasn't intending to take it."

"Yeah, okay. Or maybe she wanted one fun night before she leaves."

Wynn's eyebrows drew together. "That doesn't really sound like Abby."

"You don't think so? She goes from place to place, disaster to disaster. She's never settled down. Maybe she doesn't know how to."

From the look on Wynn's face, he realized he wasn't telling her anything she didn't know.

"Garrett, stop. You're jumping to conclusions. You don't know what she's thinking. Take her out anyway. Go out and have a good time. You *both* deserve that." She swiped a stray sprinkle off her desk. "And pretend you never heard anything about her boss's offer to go back to work."

"I'll take it under advisement, counselor." He grabbed the bag of doughnuts off her desk and walked back to his office, minus the dance steps. But maybe Wynn was right.

He wanted to spend time with Abby. Maybe they'd go on a date, decide they had nothing in common and it was best to go their separate ways. Unlikely, given their similar passions, but possible.

Also possible, they'd go on a date and she'd realize maybe it was worth a shot. Maybe *they* were worth a shot. Some of the sweetest things in his life were the ones he'd fought the hardest for.

Or maybe he was right and she was just going out with him so she could tell him in person that she was leaving.

He stabbed his fingers into his hair. So far they'd spent more time focused on Charlotte than they'd spent getting to know each other. He'd left her with a goat.

Time to regroup. He cared what happened with Abby. He liked her.

And *maybe* it was time for him to show her.

Abby dragged herself through the door of her house. She was exhausted. Elvis walked straight to his bed by the fireplace and waited for her to turn on the fire, which she did, just before she face-planted on the sofa.

How had she forgotten what school visits were like? And most of the day she'd spent seeing individual kids teachers had identified as needing a little more attention. But, along with the Comfort Dog team, she'd been on the playground and outside the school as the kids were leaving. Her introverted self was not cut out for this kind of day. She was done. Out of words.

Her phone buzzed on the coffee table, mocking her wish to just lie here with her eyes closed. Maybe she could just ignore it. The phone buzzed again, insistent. With a sigh, she rolled over and picked it up, looking at the readout. It was Garrett.

She may be close to death from sheer exhaustion, but not so close that her heart rate didn't pick up a little when she saw his name. She answered the phone. "Hey."

"Hey, you. Don't talk. I know you're tired, but I sent you something. A delivery guy just left it by your back door. He's already gone—you don't have to talk to him, either."

She smiled. *Don't talk.* It was almost as if he knew her.

"I considered flowers. But then, no one really *needs* flowers. Doughnuts, sure."

"Did you send me doughnuts?"

"No, not doughnuts. Are you following this conversation at all?"

"Garrett…" A warning tone with a hint of laughter behind it.

"Sorry, bad joke. You didn't go to the door yet?"

She rolled off the sofa and to her feet. "I'm going. Right now."

"Okay, do that. It won't keep."

Opening the back door, Abby found a box with several takeout containers inside it. She picked it up and carried it to the table, narrating as she opened the boxes. "Sweet tea, chicken potpie, a green salad, fresh yeast rolls. Garrett, you are the best." She pulled a roll from the bag and took a bite. "Comfort food is way better than flowers."

His voice sounded smug as he said, "I thought so."

With a laugh, she said, "Don't let it go to your head."

"I sent you an email, too. You can look at it later."

"Okay." She took the container of potpie, a plastic fork and the tea back to the couch with her. "How was your day?"

"I was in court this afternoon. Nash's mom got full custody of the kids again."

"That's awesome. Really good day." She took a bite. "Wow, this chicken potpie is the best thing I've eaten in decades."

"I'm glad you like it. I didn't make it."

Abby laughed again. "I figured, since there's a sticker on the container that says Hilltop Café."

"Yes, there's a clue. Okay, I'm gonna go. Enjoy your night. Sleep well. Because tomorrow is our date."

"I'll be ready."

"How does four o'clock sound? Too early?"

Four was early, but why not? "It sounds great. I'm looking forward to it."

She *was* looking forward to it. She had fun with Garrett, even if they were just exchanging quips about their day. Flipping on the television, she ate her potpie and rolls while she considered how thoughtful Garrett was. He'd realized she'd be tired and arranged the perfect thing to make her feel better.

Remembering the email, she picked up her phone and pulled it up. It was a link to a playlist. She clicked through and when she realized what it was, she laughed. Every song referred to the moon, the moonlight and stars.

It was hilarious and perfect—a subtle reminder of their kiss on her front porch under the light of that gigantic moon.

She sighed. He was goofy and silly and had the biggest heart for other people. He wasn't perfect, probably, but was he perfect for her?

Nope. She didn't need to think about that. It put too much pressure on both of them. She cared about him. They had fun together and that was good. She'd gone through all the worries in her head when she decided to go on a date in the first place. She'd come to Red Hill Springs to heal, to find the person she was…and maybe the person that she wanted to be. Letting fear get the best of her wasn't the way to do it.

No matter what happened in the future, no matter where she went, she wanted to know that she'd made the most of the time she had here, that she hadn't held herself back.

So far she'd managed to keep that promise to herself. She wasn't going to stop now.

Chapter Thirteen

"**O**uch!" Abby shook the fingers she'd just burned on the curling iron that Wynn let her borrow. She needed four hands to do this thing. How was anyone supposed to keep from getting burned when their hands were behind their head?

She hadn't curled her hair in years. Sometimes she was lucky to get to wash it. But tonight seemed special. She wanted to dress up and wear makeup and put waves in her hair. It seemed weird to her that a guy she'd seen with spit-up on his shoulder could still make her feel like a teenager getting ready for prom.

Wynn stepped into the open doorway. "Your hair looks great. It's so shiny. Want me to get the pieces you missed in the back?"

"I missed pieces… Never mind. Yes, please." Abby laughed and handed Wynn the curling iron.

Spring was definitely arriving in Alabama. Redbud trees were bursting with color. Even the grass was greening up a little bit. But since it was chilly still in March, she'd opted to wear a blouse with some lace insets, olive jeans and brown booties that she'd picked up at an end-of-season sale.

Holding out a small bag, Wynn said, "Makeup?"

"I don't even know what to do with that!"

Her friend looked at the screen on her phone and made a face. "Latham can't find Penny's soccer uniform and she has pictures tonight. I'm gonna have to run." She hugged Abby. "Have fun tonight. Be happy. You deserve it."

"It's been so good getting to spend time with you. Who knew when we were roommates in the intern dorm that we'd end up being friends for life?"

"I did." Wynn smiled. "But I'm still grateful God put us together. Call me tomorrow and let me know how it went."

"I will, I promise." Abby unzipped the makeup bag, dumped the contents onto the counter and stared at them for a minute. She picked up a large square compact and opened it. Twenty shades of eyeshadow and a small brush.

She picked the palest pink shadow and brushed it across her eyelids, peering at herself in the mirror. Okay, that made her hazel eyes kind of pop. That was a good thing, right?

Unscrewing the top on the mascara, she brushed a tiny bit on her eyelashes. Wow. Her eyes looked huge. Cool.

The next compact held blush. Her cheeks were warm already, so she dropped that back in the bag and pulled out…lip gloss. She used the wand to smooth some across her lips, took a step back, evaluated. Not bad.

The doorbell rang.

Nerves zinged in her stomach. She put her hand there and took a deep breath. It was going to be fine—fun. Fun. It was going to be *fun*.

Abby pulled the door open and Garrett stood on the porch. His hair was neatly combed and she had the urge to put her fingers in it and mess it up.

He held a bouquet of yellow wildflowers in his hand. "I rescued these from the flood. You look beautiful."

"I love them. Wait just a minute while I put them in water?"

"Sure." He stuck his hands in his pockets and took a deep breath. "It's a little bit of a drive, where we're headed. Just over an hour."

"Okay." She laid the flowers on the counter and pulled a clear pitcher from the cabinet. While it filled, she put her palms on the granite countertop and gave herself a silent pep talk. It was silly to be nervous. This was Garrett.

She cut the water off, unfolded the paper from around the flowers and put them in the pitcher. From the door, Garrett said, "Ready?"

Abby smoothed down her shirt. "Ready. Also really, really nervous. I know it's silly."

Garrett laughed. "I'm nervous, too. C'mere, I've got an idea."

She walked closer.

He linked his hand with hers with a gleam of humor in his eye. "Thumb war?"

"You're on." She suppressed a grin as she looked into his eyes. They said together, "One, two, three, four. I declare a thumb war."

Thumbs racing in circles, she stared him down until he started laughing, lost his focus and she pinned him.

Garrett's laugh burst out unrestricted. "You distracted me with the death stare. Two out of three?"

"Nope. I know how to quit while I'm ahead. Better luck next time."

"You are brutal." They left the house and walked to his SUV. He pulled open the passenger side door for her and she slid in, laughing a little as she remembered he'd said something similar when she'd made him change Charlotte's diaper the first time.

The game had done the job to dispel the tension. Her nerves were gone. In their place was the feeling that they were escaping for an adventure. That skipping-school-music-loud-windows-down kind of freedom.

She glanced over at Garrett and he flashed a grin at her and turned the music up. On the same wavelength, as usual.

It had been a long time since she felt so good. Since she'd been in Red Hill Springs, she was figuring out that she hadn't let herself find happiness—she'd been afraid of it. If she locked people out and didn't share anything with them, maybe she wouldn't get hurt.

That was no way to live.

The protective shell she'd built around her heart as a kid was slow to crumble, but Garrett's warmth and open heart had given her a reason to learn to trust again.

Garrett caught her pensive look out of the corner of his eye and turned the music down. "You got quiet all of a sudden. What are you thinking about?"

She leaned back, closer to the window. "I don't know,

just how weird it is that if you hadn't had a baby left on your doorstep, we probably wouldn't be here right now."

He drove in silence for a moment or two. "We would have met anyway. Your office is right next to mine."

"Sure, but who knows if we would've even gotten beyond pleasantries. I don't know—it's just, I wonder if Charlotte's mom had any idea what she was setting in motion."

"I don't think there's any way she could have. Mostly, I think she was trying to figure out a way to save herself."

"But even that… She wouldn't have known she could trust you unless she'd known you to be trustworthy as her guardian ad litem." Abby picked at her jeans with her fingers, but looked up with a wry smile. "I think about ripple effects sometimes. You know, I don't get to see what happens after I leave the places I work. I always pray that whatever small difference I make will ripple out in every direction."

"A tiny rock in the middle of the pond causes waves to lap against the shore." He switched lanes as they passed the welcome-to-Florida sign.

"You get the idea." Her eyebrows drew together. "Wait. We just…are those *palm trees*?"

Garrett laughed. "Yep. A friend of mine has a vacation home on Pensacola Beach and he asked me to check on it while he's out of the country. And since I had to come anyway, I thought it would be a great place to have dinner."

Her head swiveled from side to side as she took in the scenery. "I haven't been to this part of Florida in at least five years, since Hurricane Kate came through here. So much looks different."

"I wondered if you'd been back since the hurricane. I came a few times with mission teams our church sent over. There wasn't a roof spared in the whole county. On the plus side, I know how to fix a roof now."

"It looks so different. The trees were all bare and leaning over the last time I was here. It's really green now. Oh, this is so good to see."

"So you don't usually go back to the places you do disaster relief?"

"No. There just always seems to be another disaster to go to. My organization is kind of like triage or EMS. We do first aid—stem the bleeding, so to speak—until the long-term assistance organizations have time to get rolling."

He took the turn toward the beach and smiled as, once again, she let out a happy sigh.

"Kate was bad. A strong Category 3. The beach road was completely washed out. The debris, well, we couldn't even get down the roads along the water. You'd see people's clothing in the very tops of pine trees—the ones that hadn't snapped in half. Photographs scattered among the splintered wood. Bare foundations where you knew a life used to be lived."

Her voice grew husky and he reached across the armrest to take her hand. "You don't have to talk about it if you don't want to."

"It's okay. I don't mind. I think what we do has some common threads. We both come into people's lives on their worst day. And we try to make it better." Her chin trembled. "Every disaster is different. Mudslides, fires, hurricanes. But some things are the same. The way people walk around in a daze, wondering how they will overcome something so huge."

"It is huge. Literally everything is harder. So you wade in with kids and tell them…what?"

"They carry a lot of bottled-up fear and grief. So I let them talk. Remind them to look for the changes. One day something will happen… They'll be able to brush their teeth using water from the tap and they'll think today was a little easier." She was on the edge of her seat as they turned onto the beach. "This is amazing, Garrett. Thank you."

"You always see the storm. I thought you might like to see the rainbow." The houses had been rebuilt. Roads were in great condition, landscaping perfect. The beach had been restored. The dunes were slowly returning and the rosy hue of the fading sunlight made them look like they were glowing.

"That's a perfect way to put it. Thank you for bringing me here. What a gift."

He turned into a driveway and pulled to a stop under the house. "You ready?"

The house was right on the beach. He'd been coming here with his friend since he was a little kid. It had been rebuilt after the hurricane, too, and it was gorgeous, with windows across the whole width of the house, a wide porch and stairs leading down to a boardwalk.

They walked up to the porch and Abby stood next to the railing, looking out, while he set up their picnic on a small table between some loungers and started the propane heaters. With music on and string lights crisscrossing over the deck, it was cozy. Romantic. He shivered. "Wow, it's getting cold. You okay?"

She walked toward him, the breeze tossing her hair around her face. "Just awed, I think. The ocean is so peaceful and so powerful at the same time. It's amazing and awful. I've always wondered why people stay in areas like this. Why they rebuild again and again. But I can see why it's worth it."

He took her hand and tugged her closer, into the circle of warmth from the heaters. "Come on, let's sit where it's warm."

They sat cross-legged on the chaise lounges with the food between them. Abby picked up a chocolate-covered strawberry. "What about you? What gives you the ability to persevere in your job? I know it's not easy."

"Unlike you, I do get asked this a lot, like why I didn't go into corporate law, or even become a district attorney or something like that."

"And?"

"You've heard that saying, 'stand in the gap?'"

When she nodded, he said, "I think it goes back to when my parents died. I had a place to live, people who looked out for me. If I needed a place to stay, there were ten people in town I didn't even have to ask. I have a safety net a mile wide. The vast majority of people who become my clients don't have that kind of safety net. They don't have backup."

"So you stand in the gap for them." Her voice was soft.

"It sounds silly and idealistic, but yeah. Everyone needs help sometimes."

The music changed and she brushed crumbs off her fingers and held out her hand. "Come on, let's dance."

He put his hand in hers. "Okay, but I'm warning you, I'm a terrible dancer. You may have to show me."

Abby laughed. "Who, me? I can't dance."

He slid his arm around her waist. For a moment, they swayed a little, feet shuffling in time. He breathed in, letting the peace soak in as they swayed in time to the music, the percussion of the waves pounding on the sand.

Abby looked up at him, her hazel eyes dark in the dim light, full of emotion. "These last few weeks have been the best I can remember. I'm so full inside—and I was so empty when I got to Red Hill Springs. Spending time with Charlotte, soaking up those baby snuggles, and with you. Even the basic things, like going to church and having coffee with a friend. It's helped me heal. I've always known there had to be places like Red Hill Springs. I guess maybe I just thought they weren't for me."

"Is it presumptuous of me to ask if you've thought about staying?"

"I've thought about it. My boss left the option open for me to come back to work. And showing up for people when they're in crisis is important, even if it just lightens the load momentarily."

He leaned back, gave her a speculative look. "But..."

"But I want to belong somewhere." The admission slipped out. And she panicked. "You want to walk for a minute?"

"Sure."

The moon was still almost full and as it rose on the horizon, it sent waves of shimmery light across the surface of the water.

When she reached the bottom of the porch, she slid out of her shoes, stepped off into the sand and hissed. "It's so-so-so cold."

"We can stay on the porch with the nice, warm heaters."

She scoffed. "We could, but two adventurers like us? What fun would that be? Let's walk to the edge of the water. I just want to stand there for a minute."

"Of course."

It should be dark by now, but it wasn't. The moon reflected off the pure white sand. She ran for the water, hair flying out behind her, her laughter coming back to him on the wind. He chased after her, grabbing her by the waist and spinning her around, both of them laughing like children.

She pulled him toward the water where she held out her arms, letting the wind buffet her. "Wow. This is incredible."

Out of the corner of his eye, he saw something move across the sky. He put one arm around her and pointed with the other. "Look."

It was gone in a split second, that shooting burst of a star, but to Garrett it felt like it had been put there just for the two of them. She shivered and he wrapped her in his arms. She was a warrior. She went into battle for people when they were in their worst moments. But she had scars.

And his greatest desire was to stand for her, too.

Keep her safe.

But right now, her teeth were chattering. He squeezed her close and said, "Let's go. We can come back another time."

Back at the house, Abby packed up the picnic while

Garrett closed up the house and locked up, making sure the lights and music and heaters were turned off.

The ride home was more subdued than the ride out, the music a little softer. The conversation, too. Abby's eyes were on the moon as it seemed to follow them along the road.

Garrett's thoughts rambled as he drove. Abby's time in Red Hill Springs was limited. She said she felt at home, that she felt a pull to stay in Red Hill Springs, but that wasn't the same as making plans to stay.

Would they really ever come back to the beach together?

He hesitated to ask, but he really wanted to know. "Did you like your job before your last posting? Were you happy?"

She smiled. "That's such a loaded question. And the answer is I'm not sure. There was a time when I loved it, when I couldn't wait to grab my go-bag and head for the airport. Maybe I just needed some rest, to be at a place where I could rediscover the joy I felt from being with people when they needed help. Or maybe it's time for me to hang up my traveling shoes. I'm not sure yet."

"Wynn said your boss wanted you to cut your leave short and come back to work." As soon as he said it, he wanted to grab the words from the air. He hadn't meant to bring that up.

"She told you that?"

"Accidentally. She thought I knew, but yeah."

Abby made a face. "I've been avoiding my boss's calls. I've told her no twice, but disasters don't take vacations just because I do and there are only so many people like me around."

"People willing to drop their lives in a split second's notice?" He heard the edge come into his voice, a tone he didn't recognize, but one that, for some reason, had been hiding there, tucked away.

She went still and shifted ever so slightly away from him. "No. People who *live* their lives working with disaster victims."

With her arms crossed, she looked out the window and the rest of the drive was spent in uneasy silence. Garrett could feel the breach between them growing and he wanted to fix it.

When they got back to her house, he pulled into the drive and parked. "Abby, I didn't mean to be disrespectful. I misspoke and I'm sorry."

"It's fine," she said, but her body language said it was anything but.

"It's not fine. I don't think you had no life before you came here. What a presumption that would be. But I hurt you and I'd never do that intentionally."

"It's fine." She opened the door. "I really did have a good time. Thank you for taking me."

He met her on her side of the vehicle and walked her to the door. He wanted to snap his fingers and return them to the way they felt when they were dancing. He leaned forward and gave her a rather unsatisfying kiss—on the cheek, as she turned her head.

He got back in the car and waited for her to close the door before he slammed his hand on the steering wheel. He'd offended Abby. And he was pretty sure he'd blown any chance he had of convincing her to stay in Red Hill Springs.

Chapter Fourteen

Abby found Lacey on her doorstep the next morning. She opened the door and waved her friend inside. "Why am I not surprised to see you here?"

Lacey plopped her purse onto the kitchen table and pulled out one of the chairs while Abby took another mug out of the kitchen cabinet. "Cream?"

"Yes, please."

Setting the mug of coffee and carton of cream on the table in front of Lacey, Abby joined her at the table. "Okay, what's up?"

Lacey tried to give her an innocent look but gave up after about half a second. "Okay, fine. I have to know what happened with you and Garrett last night. He left home like he was on cloud nine, but this morning he just about bit Devin's head off. Abby, I like you, but if you broke Garrett's heart, I'm gonna have to hurt you."

Abby nearly choked on her coffee. She had a feeling she was seeing rodeo Lacey, who had the nerve to barrel race at champion speed. "Glad to know where I stand. We had a great time. It was a beautiful night."

"But?"

"I thought we ended things okay last night, but Garrett hurt my feelings and I guess I showed it."

"You're going to get over it, though?"

That was the million-dollar question, wasn't it? She cared about Garrett, but if he was going to get his back up every time she had to go out of town, they wouldn't be able to take this relationship to the next level.

She sighed. "Honestly, I'm not sure I'm relationship material. Not everyone is like you and Devin."

Lacey laughed. "Thank God for that. We almost got a divorce before the twins were born. If Devin hadn't had the sense to fight for the relationship, we would have."

"Are you joking?" Abby gaped at Lacey. "But he's so—and you're so—"

"He's so good-looking? Charming? Talented? Yeah, he's all those things, but he was—is—also an addict and he did some really awful things, like leaving me the morning after our wedding night."

"I'm floored."

Lacey's revelation was truly shocking, but if the two of them had survived that kind of trouble, maybe there was hope for her and Garrett. Assuming there even *was* a her and Garrett.

"By God's grace, Devin convinced me to give him a second chance. To give *us* a second chance." Lacey picked up her mug and held it between her hands. "Loving someone—truly loving them—isn't easy. Even if you think you've met the perfect person, they're not perfect. Everyone has flaws. If you don't see them, you're just blinded by infatuation. Real love sees the flaws and decides to love anyway."

Abby sat quietly in her chair. She didn't like hearing it, but Lacey was right. "He said he was sorry. I think he knew immediately that he hurt my feelings."

"What did he say?" Lacey asked gently.

"He implied that I didn't have a life because I travel all the time. But I chose to live my life that way." She shook her head. "I know it's a fine distinction, but it's an important one. The thing is, I think what he said hit so close to home because I've wondered the same thing. Have I spent all these years running from job to job because I don't know how to find peace?"

Lacey leaned toward her. "You do something not many people could do. You lend your strength to people who've used theirs all up."

Abby swallowed hard around the lump in her throat. "Thanks."

Lacey reached across the table and gripped Abby's hand. "But it's okay for you to need to borrow some strength when you need it, too."

A tear streaked down Abby's face and she scrubbed it away, horrified. "Sorry. I don't know what's the matter with me."

"Nothing is wrong with you." Lacey's voice was firm. "You have emotions. It happens."

"Not to me." Abby laughed through her tears.

"To you *and* to Garrett. He's steady as a rock. Funny and sweet and would give his last dollar to anyone— literally anyone—who needed it."

"Now I feel a *but* coming on."

A smile flitted across Lacey's face. "The car accident that took their parents and Tanner's wife and baby— no one could survive that and come out unscathed.

Garrett has an amazing heart, but I wonder sometimes what he's hiding behind all that generosity."

"You think he's afraid of…really caring?"

"I don't know. You're the professional—I'm just an armchair psychologist—but they lost a lot that day, all three of them."

Abby took a deep breath and used those few seconds to settle herself. "What you're saying makes sense. I need to think about it a little bit more."

Her phone buzzed on the table and she glanced at the screen. Her boss again, but this time, the text just said, 911.

Abby's stomach dropped. That kind of text could only be bad. She excused herself and walked outside to make the call. A few minutes later, she returned to the kitchen.

Lacey looked up. "It's bad news, isn't it?"

"There was an earthquake this morning in California. A school was damaged and children are trapped in the building. Elvis and I have to go."

Elvis's tail thumped on the floor and, though Abby's heart was breaking, she reached down to scratch his head. He was always ready to go. His big heart never got tired.

Lacey hugged Abby. "I'll be praying—for the kids and for you. And I'll see you when you get back."

"Thanks, Lacey." She walked Lacey to the door and pushed it closed behind her, before looking back at Elvis. "Time to pack, buddy. We're on the 3:00 p.m. flight."

A few hours later, Abby stood in the kitchen, running through her mental list. She'd called Wynn, arranged to be away, packed their necessities. She hated to leave, especially leaving things with Garrett the way they were, but she was needed and it was time to go.

Stepping out onto the porch, she let Elvis go through the door before she moved to lock it. When she turned back, Garrett was standing in the driveway, leaning on her car.

Her stomach flipped. He looked miserable. Which, she guessed, was fitting because she felt pretty miserable about how their date ended last night, too.

She stopped about a foot away, facing him. "Hi."

"Lacey told me you got called in for the earthquake in California. I wasn't sure what to do, but I knew I didn't want you to leave without talking to you first." Garrett looked over her shoulder and back again. "I brought you some snacks for the plane."

She couldn't help it—she started to laugh. "You really have a compulsive need to take care of people, don't you?"

"Maybe I need therapy." He smiled, but his eyes, which were usually so full of life, didn't reflect it. "I really don't want you to go. And, trust me, I know how selfish that sounds."

"I wish I didn't have to go, too." She lifted her shoulders. "But it's what I do."

"I know. I'm proud of you for doing it, too, even though it worries me."

The uneasy knot she'd been carrying since last night loosened a little. "Why are you worried?"

"I feel like we're just getting started and I'm not ready to say goodbye."

She wanted to reach out to him, to reassure him that

she would always come back, but the truth was she couldn't predict what was going to happen.

Instead, she touched his hand. "I have to come back—I left Elvis's bed here. He'd never forgive me."

"I'll count on it." He smiled then and handed her a gallon-sized plastic bag full of trail mix, candy bars and peanut butter crackers.

"This should get me to Atlanta, at least."

His eyes on hers, he slid his fingers into her hair but he didn't kiss her. She could see the need—she could feel it in herself, too. The connection between them had been there from almost the very beginning.

She leaned forward and pressed her lips to his. "I'll see you in a few days."

Four days passed, then six, as Garrett got moodier and moodier. Devin threatened to punch him more than once. Tanner suggested that maybe he could find a place to live back in town. Charlotte didn't care if he was grumpy. Which is why she was his favorite.

He'd followed the news coverage of the earthquake, even catching a glimpse of Abby in the background of a picture someone had taken of the Comfort Dog team, who was also in California.

Every night at ten o'clock, he sent her a picture of Charlotte—the cutest, sweetest one he could find. And unlike Brooklyn, Abby always texted him back. The first night she'd texted, I know what you're doing and it's totally working. I miss you guys.

He should've guessed that she'd see through him, but he kept sending the pictures because he wanted contact with her. He asked her how she was doing, and she always said tired, but doing good. And he wasn't sure if she meant that she was feeling okay or that she was actually participating in doing good. Either way, she had to be exhausted, so he kept the conversations light and short.

On day eight, he sat in the porch swing on the front porch of the farmhouse, rocking Charlotte. He'd picked her up early because the day care workers said she was fussy and wasn't taking a bottle. She'd taken a couple of ounces from him, but her nose was stuffy and she still wasn't happy.

The door opened and Lacey stuck her head out. "Hey, supper's almost ready. Why don't you come inside?"

"Devin said I couldn't come over anymore."

"When Devin cooks, Devin can decide who comes over for dinner."

Garrett shifted Charlotte to his shoulder and stood. "Sounds logical to me."

He was sitting at the table with Charlotte beside him in her swing when Devin walked in from the back porch. Devin stopped halfway through the door and growled, "All right, but if you moan and groan the whole time you're here, you're gonna have to leave."

Garrett buttered his biscuit calmly. "I promise."

Tanner came in and poured himself a glass of tea. He didn't say anything, just sat down at the table and picked up a biscuit. The twins were in their high chairs. Lacey handed each of them a cold teething ring, sat down at the table and held out her hands. "Let's pray."

All four of them bowed their heads. Their mom had always insisted on saying grace before meals and they'd continued the practice even after her passing. Lacey finished the prayer. Devin said amen. And Charlotte sneezed.

Garrett's head snapped up. "What was that?"

"It was just a little sneeze." Lacey patted his hand and held out a platter. "Pork chop?"

He stabbed one with his fork. "Parenting stinks."

"No. Uh-uh." Devin pointed at the door. "Out. I warned you."

Garrett blinked mildly. "Lacey invited me."

"It's true, I did. Garrett, mind your manners. Abby will be home soon."

Tanner looked up. "For all our sakes, I hope that's true."

"*Et tu*, Tanner?" Garrett took a bite of his pork chop and heard a tiny cough from the swing. He glanced over to check on Charlotte and noticed her cheeks were bright pink. "Uh, Lacey, she doesn't look very good."

Lacey took a good look at the baby and stood up. "I'll go get the thermometer."

Garrett's heart started racing as Charlotte coughed again. This was the part of parenting that he hated. The part where you had no idea what to do and every decision counted.

Lacey ran the thermometer across Charlotte's forehead. The screen flashed red. Garrett didn't know much about sick babies, but flashing red couldn't be good. Lacey looked up, concern on her face. "I think you better call Ash. Her temp is 104."

Devin shoved back from the table. "I'll get the baby fever reducer."

Tanner stood, too. "I'll get a cool washcloth."

Charlotte started to cry, but it ended in a wheezy

cough. Garrett lifted her into his arms. Her tiny body was burning up.

He dialed the phone, spoke to Ash and then turned to his brothers. "Can one of y'all get the car? He said he'd meet us at the ER."

Three hours later, Garrett was still waiting in a tiny cubicle in the ER. Charlotte had been crying for an hour and had finally exhausted herself, falling into a restless sleep. He'd been on pins and needles waiting for word from the doctors about what was going on.

He was worried. On a regular day, he tried to pretend it was normal that his heart was wrapped up in this baby girl's tiny fist, but today, he couldn't do it. He needed to know she would be okay.

The door opened and the emergency room doctor came in, followed by Ash. Dr. Seagar sat on the rolling stool and pulled the computer monitor closer to him. "Okay, so we have some results for you. Charlotte's chest X-ray is normal, which is good. She doesn't have pneumonia. She's a little dehydrated from not taking in very much fluid today, but that's easily treatable. Her flu test was negative."

"She was positive for RSV." Ash pushed off the wall where he'd been leaning, his hands going to the pockets of his white coat and pulling out a brochure and sliding it onto the bed.

"What's RSV?" Garrett looked down into Charlotte's little face. Her cheeks were pink, hair a little sweaty and stuck to her head. Her breathing was fast and raspy.

"Respiratory Syncytial Virus. In adults and older kids, RSV isn't any worse than the common cold, but in small babies, RSV can be dangerous because it can worsen quickly. Charlotte has bronchiolitis and the wheezing and high fever make me a little nervous about sending her home."

"You're going to admit her?" Garrett unconsciously squeezed Charlotte a little tighter.

"Not necessarily. If you're dead set on taking her home—"

"No." Garrett interrupted Ash. "If you think she needs admitting, then admit her. I'm not going to argue about that."

"If she were three months older..." Ash's statement trailed off. He tucked the eartips of his stethoscope into his ears and placed the round part on Charlotte's back, listening for a minute before taking it off and curling it back into his pocket. "As it is, I'd feel better if we keep her overnight, get some fluids in her and support her with oxygen. You agree with that, Dr. Seagar?"

"I do. Breathing treatments will help the wheezing and we can check her again tomorrow for developing pneumonia."

Garrett knew they were talking and he heard them say they wanted to go ahead and admit her, but the words dwindled away, replaced by a roaring sound in his ears.

Seagar left the room. Ash placed a hand on Garrett's shoulder. "Call me if you need anything. I'll check on y'all tomorrow."

"What happens now?" His voice came out hoarse.

Ash leaned against the counter. "They'll send someone from Admission in to go over the paperwork with you. They'll give both you and Charlotte new ID bands.

Then they'll send a transporter down to take you upstairs to the room."

"Can I stay with her?" Charlotte stirred in his arms, whimpered and the sound turned into a wheezy cough.

"Yes, of course. There's a chair that folds out into a bed in the room. She's in good hands, Garrett."

A woman wearing a hospital badge came in the door rolling a computer. Ash squeezed his shoulder one final time and left.

When the seemingly endless paperwork was finished, a volunteer walked him and Charlotte up to the second floor and handed them over to the nurse at the desk.

She was an older lady with gray-blond hair pulled into a knot at the back of her head. "I'm Susan. This must be Charlotte. We've got a room ready for you."

The walls of the hall were painted in a jungle theme, with happy monkeys, giraffes, tigers and lions. He personally didn't think children would want to see happy predators when they were in the hospital, but what did he know? He'd been a dad for six weeks now and his baby was in the hospital. He cleared his throat. "She hasn't eaten in a while. She might need a bottle."

In lieu of an answer, the nurse held her hands out for Charlotte. "I'll take her now."

Lawyer that he was, he couldn't hand Charlotte over without comment. "Why?"

"We're going to get her IV started and get her hooked up to the monitors. Trust me, you don't want to be in here for this part."

He kissed Charlotte on her warm little head with its peach-fuzz hair and passed her to the nurse. Charlotte started to cry, which Garrett understood because he was barely holding it together as he stood outside the door to the room. He only had a vague idea of what was going on in the room, but Charlotte was screaming louder and more vehemently than he'd ever heard her, the kind of cry that went straight to his gut.

Maybe he should be in there. Maybe he wasn't cut out to be Charlotte's dad. The thought that something could happen to her shattered him.

A few minutes later, a different nurse in pink scrubs with yellow ducks on the top came out the door, pulling off gloves and a mask. This nurse smiled. "Charlotte's dad?"

"Yes." Where was his baby?

"I'm Lucy. I'm Charlotte's nurse tonight. Don't worry, she's doing fine. We'll have her settled in just a few minutes. There's a family room at the end of the hall. You can get a drink and a snack if you'd like. This would be a good time to call who you need to call to let them know Charlotte will be in the hospital for a few days."

"A few days?"

She paused in the doorway. "Typically, when we have babies admitted for RSV, they stay a few days, but it's just a guess."

The crying had waned. Charlotte's raspy cry didn't sound angry anymore, just pitiful. "I don't want to leave her."

"Get something to drink. Take a breather. She's going to need you to be strong for her." Nurse Lucy went back into the room and he stood there for a moment staring at the door. If the two nurses were playing good cop–bad cop, this one was definitely the good cop. But he took her advice and went down the hall to find a vending machine.

Then he had to call Brooklyn. It was a call he dreaded.

More than anything, he wanted to call Abby. He'd give anything to see her walk through that door, but she was in California and already exhausted. It might make him feel better to talk to her, but it would only make things harder for her.

He needed her calm confidence right now.

He needed her.

The thought knocked him back.

In the space of two months, he'd gone from single bachelor, no kids, to being the dad of a two-month-old he'd give his life for in a hot second. And on top of that, he was in love with...

He staggered against the wall of the hospital and buried his face in his hands. The truth was right there in front of him. He'd fallen in love with Abby.

Everything was spinning out of control. Two months ago, he'd been content with his life, before a tiny baby and a strong-willed woman had shown him just how much he'd been missing. Now, Charlotte was struggling for breath. Abby was gone. And he was facing losing both of them.

Even if he'd never gotten over it, he'd managed to get through the loss of his parents. But the thought of losing Charlotte and Abby rocked him to the core.

And he didn't know how he could possibly live through it.

Chapter Fifteen

Abby rushed in the doors of the hospital and up the stairs to the second floor, Elvis at her side. When her flight arrived at the airport in Mobile, she'd gotten a text message from Wynn that Charlotte was in the hospital and she'd headed straight here.

Her heart was in her throat. Sweet baby girl. Abby couldn't bear the thought of her being sick.

Stopping at the nurse's desk to check in with Elvis, she asked for directions to Charlotte's room. A nurse named Lucy pointed her down the hall.

When she arrived, the door was slightly open. She could see Garrett sitting in a chair, his face in his hands. Softly, she said, "Elvis, go say hello."

Elvis streaked across the room to Garrett, stuck his head between Garrett's arms and nuzzled. Garrett's head shot up as his arms closed around Elvis, his eyes searching for hers.

She smiled even as she felt her eyes prick with tears. Despite the circumstances, she was happy to see him. Glad she could be here for him.

Abby stepped into the room, her gaze going to Charlotte, who was asleep in a crib under the only light in the room. Her arm was wrapped in a splint to protect her IV, her lower leg encircled in a blood pressure cuff. On the opposite big toe was the glowing red light of the pulse oximeter and in her nose, a tiny nasal cannula delivering oxygen so her body didn't have to work so hard.

Abby reached Charlotte's side and brushed her fingers across the downy soft hair. "Oh, baby girl."

Garrett walked to the end of the bed. "She's holding her own. They gave her something to bring her fever down and she's been sleeping."

Resisting the urge to throw herself into his arms and sob, Abby blew out a breath. She'd been at the bedside of literally hundreds of children and never shed a tear because it was her job to hold it together. But Charlotte was hers—even if she wasn't, not really.

"When did she get sick?"

"I noticed she had a stuffy nose yesterday. She didn't sleep well last night. They called me from day care and said she hadn't been eating, so I picked her up early. She started coughing at dinner tonight and her fever was 104."

"Oh, Garrett. How scary."

"We haven't been in the room very long, just long enough for them to get her settled and for me to realize what's at stake here."

"I'm so sorry. Can I hug you?"

The words were barely out of her mouth before he pulled her into his arms, burying his face in her hair. "I missed you. How did you even know to come?"

"I was on a plane already. Wynn texted me and I got it when I landed. I came straight here."

"I'm so thankful." He let her go but kept his arm around her as they stood at the side of Charlotte's crib.

"Can we pray for her? Will you?" He placed his hand on Charlotte's foot while she kept hers on the downy head.

Abby's voice shook with emotion as the words poured out. "Papa God, You are our Father, always watching out for us, caring for us in ways we can't even understand. We know You watch over Charlotte, too. Please lend her Your strength to fight off this illness. Protect her from harm. Be with Garrett. He needs Your peace and Your wisdom right now more than ever. And thank You, God, for never leaving us alone to face our hardships. Amen."

"Amen." Garrett cleared his throat. "I'm glad you came."

"I can stay, but if you'd rather try to sleep while she's sleeping, I'll go."

"Please stay?"

She dragged a visitor's chair across the room so she could sit next to Garrett. "So other than ending up in the hospital, how was your week?"

Unbelievably, he chuckled. "Terrible. Devin threatened to punch me. Tanner wanted to kick me out."

"Oh, no!"

His smile faded. "I missed you. How was yours?"

"It was good to be back at work, but this deployment was intense. All of them are, I guess, but because the children were trapped, this one seemed more so. I guess you saw on the news that they got them all out?"

"I did. And you got to visit with them?"

"Yes. They were really brave and funny. Reminded me of Nash. You would've loved them."

"I would."

"I fell right back in the rhythm of things. Red Hill Springs felt like a weird, wonderful dream."

"I was afraid you'd get back to work and wouldn't want to come back." His eyes were on Charlotte, on the monitors which, though silent, recorded every heartbeat, every breath.

"I needed to come back." She hesitated to say more, not because she didn't understand how he was feeling, but because it wasn't the time to talk about her feelings, not with so much at stake here.

His face was scruffy, eyes tired as he looked back at her. She'd had some time to think in California, but she wasn't ready to talk about it yet. Not until things were certain and definitely not until Charlotte was better.

"I called Brooklyn. She didn't answer so I left a message. Then I texted her. I'm not sure what else to do." Garrett yawned and squinted at his watch. "I'm exhausted. We didn't sleep much last night and I blew through a ton of energy when I realized how sick she was."

"Why don't you sit down and sleep for a while? I'll keep watch."

He held his hand out and she slid hers into it, trying not to make a big deal out of how natural it felt to do so. Their relationship wasn't a given, not by a long shot, but she'd been with Garrett and Charlotte since the beginning and being here felt right.

As his eyes closed, hers were drawn to Charlotte, the rapid rise and fall of her tiny little chest. *Please God, let her be okay.*

* * *

Garrett woke with a start, rubbed his gritty eyes and stumbled to his feet. He needed coffee. The agonizingly slow night had finally turned to daylight. He'd tried for hours to comfort Charlotte after the nurses had to suction her nose and mouth around one o'clock in the morning.

He looked over toward the crib. Abby was in the reclining chair, where she'd finally settled millimeter by millimeter with Charlotte on her chest after the baby had fallen into a fitful sleep. Elvis, on the floor beside her, lifted his head to watch Garrett, but didn't move.

None of them had gotten more than an hour or two of rest. The one thing he could say on the positive was that Charlotte seemed to be breathing a little bit easier now that she wasn't dehydrated and was getting supplemental oxygen. The nurse had told him in the middle of the night that Charlotte wouldn't be able to leave the hospital until her fever was gone and she could take a bottle and keep it down.

Garrett slid his feet into his shoes and picked up Elvis's leash from the counter. "Come on, boy, let's go outside."

Elvis's tail thumped but he didn't stir from Abby's side. Garrett shrugged. "Okay, your call."

Pulling open the door to the hall, he stopped short, face-to-face with a young girl with bright pink hair that matched her high-top tennis shoes. The hair stood up on the back of his neck.

Brooklyn. Charlotte's mother.

He physically took a step back, before he closed the

door and stepped into the hall, still trying to process her presence. "Wow, hey."

He studied her face. She looked good. Tired, but better than he did, for sure.

Her chin came up. "I'm not using."

"Good. Come on, let's go get a cup of coffee. I'm about to fall over and I want to be back before the doctor comes for rounds."

She glanced wistfully at the door, but followed him. "How is she? I got in the car as soon as I got your text."

"She's not critical, but she's not good."

"I don't know what that means."

"She needs support to get over the virus she has because she's so little. You know, tubes and IVs and monitors and stuff." He stopped walking. "I can't believe I'm just standing here having a conversation with you. Where have you been?"

"I know you have a lot of questions. I'll get to the answers, I promise. Just please, tell me about Charlotte."

"It's serious, but she should be fine. Most babies with this go home in about a week." He repeated what the nurses had told him, trying to infuse the words with more confidence than he felt.

"A week? I'll get kicked out of school if I stay a week."

"You're in school?"

She reached a hand up and self-consciously touched a lock of cotton-candy-colored hair. "Cosmetology school."

He held the door to the cafeteria open for her. "Last time I checked, we had cosmetology school right here."

Technically, he had no idea if that was true. He'd

never checked to see if there were cosmetology schools in Alabama. He walked over to the cafeteria line and pointed at a sausage biscuit. "Two, please. Do you want anything?"

"No, thanks."

He paid the cashier for the biscuits and two cups of coffee, walked to a table and sat down, assuming Brooklyn would follow him. She paid for her own cup of coffee and sat down across from him.

"Why don't you start at the beginning?"

Her eyes were big and round, the same dark blue as Charlotte's. She didn't have the benefit of growing up in a family like his, with the moral compass of his father. And he reminded himself to show her compassion. She deserved that, no matter how bad her decisions had been.

"You know I was hanging out with a rough crowd when I was aging out of foster care."

"I had that idea, yes."

She twisted the foam cup in her hands. "They were—are—pretty hard users. I was, too, when I was with them. But when I found out I was pregnant with Charlotte, I stopped."

"Who's the father?"

Her cheeks colored and she looked away. "I don't know."

"Okay. Go on."

"I couldn't figure out how I could stay clean. Once she came, I couldn't stay at the pregnancy shelter anymore and I knew if I went to any of my so-called friends, I'd be back in the same place I was before I started. I knew I needed to make a clean break."

"Why didn't you ask me for help?"

"That's a question I've asked myself a billion times. And I don't know. I guess I was embarrassed. And desperate. Would you really have said yes to Charlotte if I had asked you?"

She had a point. He wouldn't have. He might have found a place for Charlotte, maybe even for both of them, but he wouldn't have taken her. He took a slow sip of the hot coffee. It tasted terrible.

He took another sip and sighed. "I get why you left. I even understand it. But I don't understand why you couldn't make contact with me after you left."

"I thought you'd be mad or try to convince me to come home." Her eyes were pleading with him to understand. "Garrett, I can't come back here. There's a way for me to make a better life. I'm so close. I know it'll be hard but I need to do this. I won't make it if I stay here."

Garrett was too tired to argue. Too tired to come up with a creative solution. Too tired, period.

He stood and tossed his empty coffee cup into the trash can and picked up his uneaten biscuit and the coffee and biscuit he'd bought for Abby. "All right, let's go."

Brooklyn's footsteps seemed to get slower and heavier the closer they got to the room. "I don't know if I can do this."

"My friend Abby's been helping me with Charlotte. She's in there with her now."

Brooklyn stopped, tears brimming in her eyes. "What if Charlotte hates me?"

He put an arm around her shoulders. "Then you'll really be a parent. You came all this way to check on her—at least come in and see her."

* * *

"Hi." Abby looked up as the door opened. Garrett paused halfway through. "Is that coffee? You might be my hero."

She looked down at Charlotte, who squirmed but didn't wake up. "The nurse came in a few minutes ago to check on her and said they'd be coming back to do some blood work."

"Fabulous news."

"They want you to try a bottle with her and see if she'll take it." They'd tried a bottle twice during the night and both times, Charlotte had not been able to keep it down.

"Abby?"

Something in the tone of his voice made her look up again and she realized he wasn't alone. As he stepped into the room, a young girl with pink hair crept in behind him.

"Sorry, I didn't realize we had company. Hi, I'm Abby."

Silence stretched for a long few seconds. Garrett nudged the girl forward.

"I'm Brooklyn. Charlotte's, um, mom."

Only long years of practice schooling her expression enabled Abby to say with a smile, "It's nice to finally meet you in person."

After another nudge from Garrett, Brooklyn muttered her thanks.

Despite trying to give Brooklyn the benefit of the doubt all along, Abby's feelings had ping-ponged from judgment to compassion and back again. When she saw Charlotte's mom in person, though, all those mixed feelings vanished. All she could see was a terrified teen, trying to do the best for her baby in the only way she knew how.

"Take a look, B." Garrett edged her forward. "She won't bite."

"She looks so sick," Brooklyn whispered.

"She *is* sick." Abby found Garrett's eyes with hers before going back to Brooklyn. "But they're taking really good care of her here. Why don't you wash up at the sink and you can hold her?"

Brooklyn took a step back. "I don't know. She's not used to me. And all those wires and tubes..."

Garrett's eyebrows drew together into a frown. Abby could tell that he was hanging on to decorum by a thin thread. She quickly said, "You came all this way to see her. It would be a shame if you didn't try."

Brooklyn dropped her backpack in a chair, moved to the sink and turned the water on. Garrett mouthed, "Sorry."

Abby lifted a shoulder and shook her head.

Once Brooklyn had used the hand sanitizer and stood awkwardly waving her hands in the air to dry them, Abby eased to a standing position. Garrett helped her untangle herself from the wires recording Charlotte's vital signs.

She sent Brooklyn a reassuring smile. "Come on over. You sit in the chair and I'll put her in your arms. Garrett, you want to hand Brooklyn one of those gowns to put on over her clothes?"

While Brooklyn slid the gown on, Abby had a chance to study her. Hands were steady. Eyes and skin clear, if tired. She really seemed to be free of drugs.

Abby silently prayed that God would support this young girl, who just seemed so lost.

With a trembling smile, Brooklyn sat in the chair. "Y'all are sure this is okay? I'm so nervous."

"It's perfectly fine, but if she cries, it's not you. It's because she's not feeling well and she hasn't been very tolerant of being handled." As slowly and gently as she could, Abby moved Charlotte into Brooklyn's arms.

Charlotte let out a small cry that quickly turned into a wheezing cough. Brooklyn's head jerked up, her eyes widening in alarm.

"She's okay. Give it a minute." Garrett's jaw clenched, his features strung tight.

Abby touched her eye. Elvis had already been watching her closely as the tension grew in the room. He rose to a sitting position, his ears perking up. She pointed at Garrett. "Rest."

Elvis trotted across the room and sat as close to Garrett's legs as possible, leaning into them. Garrett's hand dropped to rub the dog's head and he took a deep breath.

Good boy, Elvis.

It was totally natural that Garrett would feel protective of Charlotte, even angry at Brooklyn. She'd taken advantage of a professional relationship, plunging it into the personal the moment she'd left the baby on Garrett's porch. But right now, their focus had to be on Charlotte.

Brooklyn being here was a huge answer to prayer. Maybe Garrett could get all of his questions answered. Maybe all of them could see this through to a resolution that made sense. But it all—every bit of it—hinged on Brooklyn's next steps.

Abby stripped out of the hospital gown she'd been

wearing over her own clothes. She stopped next to Garrett. His eyes didn't move from Charlotte.

Tears ran down Brooklyn's face.

It was time for Abby to go. She'd done everything she could to help Garrett and now he and Brooklyn had to work things out. Abby might be a buffer for the tension, but they were going to have to figure out how to talk without her, for Charlotte's sake.

Her purse and Elvis's leash were on the counter and she picked them up. "I need to go home for a while. Elvis needs a break. I'll text you later."

Panic flared in Garrett's eyes but he didn't say anything. She gave him a quick hug with Elvis between them and left the room.

When the door closed behind her, she rubbed a hand across her eyes. Garrett's pain and confusion and worry was hard to handle. She wanted to take it away, to fix it. But that wasn't her job.

Being in California had clarified a few things for her. She loved her job, but she needed roots. She was fine alone, but she needed family—even if it was one she created for herself. And being independent was great, but as much as she'd tried to keep Garrett firmly in the friend column, she'd done the one thing she'd always said she never would.

She'd fallen in love.

And now her heart was in his hands.

Chapter Sixteen

Garrett watched Brooklyn's face soften with love. His jaw clenched tighter. He wasn't even sure how to feel at this point. He wanted to believe she'd do what was best for Charlotte, but how could he know that?

After all of this, if Brooklyn changed her mind and decided to take Charlotte, what choice did he have but to let her? Yes, Charlotte was in his temporary legal custody, but only because Brooklyn had signed it over to him.

He was exhausted. Worried because Charlotte was sick. And more than a little desperate. In one horribly unfair accident, he'd lost his parents, his sister-in-law, his baby niece, and for all practical purposes, his brothers. How could he stand it if he lost Charlotte?

And Abby? With her back doing disaster relief, he wasn't sure Abby wasn't already gone.

His breath hitched out and his lungs refused to draw in another one. Brooklyn glanced up at him. "What's wrong? You look like you're about to have a heart attack."

"Are you planning on taking Charlotte back?" The question was so weighted that it seemed to hang in the air. He couldn't hear a thing over the roaring in his ears as he waited for her answer.

She ducked her head, a lock of candy-colored hair falling into her eyes as she looked down at Charlotte. "Maybe one day I'll be ready to be a mom. I hope so. I love her more than anything. I know that's probably hard to believe, but it's true. The second I saw her…"

Her voice broke and he had to fight hard to squelch the urge to let his questions go. But he needed answers. Charlotte needed answers. "But?"

Brooklyn squirmed under his scrutiny. "I can't take care of anyone else until I can take care of myself. I want you to raise her. She needs a real family. You have the paperwork, right?"

He nodded slowly. "There's one thing you didn't consider. I'm a mandatory reporter. I had to tell Child Services that you left her."

Her mouth gaped open, angry tears instantly in her eyes, her voice a hot whisper. "She's in *foster* care? I trusted you!"

"Calm down and let me finish, please." Somehow he'd ended up as a father figure to this eighteen-year-old girl. She *had* trusted him and maybe what she'd done was unfathomable to the average Joe, but to him—knowing what had happened to her and all that she'd been through—it made a sad kind of sense. "I convinced the judge to let her stay with me. She's been with me all along."

"Okay." Brooklyn closed her eyes and took a deep

breath, the word tumbling out again as she let it go. "Okay."

He crossed his arms. "But I need to hear you say what you intend to do now."

She hesitated and in that split second, the door opened.

The daytime nurse, Darla, came in with a perky smile. "Time for vitals. I need to draw some blood and then we're going to try a bottle."

The color drained from Brooklyn's face. "Come get her, Garrett."

"She's doing fine with you."

The color drained from her cheeks. "Garrett, please. Come get her."

Taking pity on her, Garrett crossed the room to the chair where she was sitting by the crib. His hands sure, he lifted Charlotte from Brooklyn's arms. The baby squirmed and her cold-swollen eyes squinted up at him.

He smiled down at her. "Hey, sweet girl."

She opened her mouth and wailed—a raspy cry which brought on a coughing fit. He wished with everything he had he could take her sickness from her, that he was the one in the hospital instead of her.

The nurse pulled the tray of instruments to a spot within her reach. "She really doesn't like being moved, does she? Okay, Dad, hold her in your lap, with her head against your chest and wrap your arm around, yep, just like that." She looked up at Brooklyn. "Can you grab a toy and try to distract her? We use a tiny little butterfly needle. It won't be bad. She may not even cry."

Brooklyn froze, a deer in the headlights. She blinked a couple of times and then ran from the room.

Garrett sighed. "Sorry. Just go ahead. I've got Charlotte."

Charlotte cried, but Garrett thought it was more that she was mad and hungry and hated being held down than the needle stick. That part was over fast thanks to Nurse Darla with the steady hands.

Darla stuck a cartoon character bandage over Charlotte's boo-boo. "She's good to go. The doctor wants the results before he does rounds, so I'm going to run this down to be processed and I'll be right back with a bottle."

Garrett turned Charlotte toward his chest and held her close, gently patting her back. She was so tiny to be going through such a rough time.

Her hoarse cries broke his heart.

He haltingly began to sing her favorite Beatles song about holding hands and her cries began to lessen. When she finally stopped crying, he eased her onto the bed and kept singing, grabbing a clean diaper from the drawer and changing her as she watched him with her dark blue eyes.

Her little chin wrinkled, the bottom lip poking out as he fastened the last tab and picked her up. "All done. You are such a good girl. And you have good taste in music."

When he turned around, Brooklyn was standing in the door, tears drying on her cheeks. "I'm sorry. I couldn't stand seeing her that way."

"It's okay. I don't like it either."

"But you did it. You're a really great dad." She paused and looked down at her pink tennis shoes. "You asked me if I was planning to take Charlotte back. The answer's no. It's always been no, but if I had any question about it, I don't anymore."

"Brooklyn... I want you to be sure."

She nodded and said, almost too quiet for him to hear, "I wish I had a dad like you."

Her words cut straight to his heart. He'd known her a long time. And he was the one who'd been the most stable influence in her life. He quirked a finger at her. "Come here."

With Charlotte between them, he put his arm around Brooklyn. "You do have me. You're not alone."

She laid her head with her cotton-candy hair on his shoulder and wept. His heart broke for this sweet young woman, who hadn't been loved the way she deserved by the people who were supposed to love her.

When she finally stepped back, he said, "I mean it, Brooklyn. You might've aged out of foster care on your own, but you're not on your own now."

Twin tears tracked down her cheeks. "Why aren't you mad at me?"

He shrugged, but he looked down at Charlotte, the blush of strawberry-blond hair, long blond eyelashes fanning across her cheek—almost invisible unless you looked really close. She'd changed his life for the better in so many ways. "I think you believed you were making the best choice for you and for Charlotte. I may not like how you went about it, but I understand it."

Brooklyn's cheeks puffed out as she blew out a breath. "I'm wrecked. I need to go wash my face and then I really have to get back to Nashville."

"That's where you are? Nashville?"

She nodded. "It's far enough away that I don't know

anyone. Close enough that I don't feel like I'm living in a foreign country."

"Before you go, I need you to do something."

The wariness returned to her eyes and he was reminded again that she'd experienced things in her short eighteen years that no person should have to. Her reactions to things were extreme because she'd lived a life of extremes.

"It's not bad, but I need to get sworn testimony from you about your intentions when you left Charlotte with me. The only alternative to doing that would be to come back when we have court."

"I can't come back. I need to get my degree."

"Okay. Let's see if we can get Charlotte to take a bottle while we wait for Abby. I'll call my office and see if I can get someone in to take a sworn statement and one of the caseworkers from the Department of Human Resources to witness it, so they can testify in court." He tugged his phone out of his pocket and texted Abby to see where she was.

When he looked up, Brooklyn's eyes were intent on his. "I'm glad I came today."

"Me, too."

"Did you mean what you said about me having family now?" She looked down at her hands, twisting together in a fruitless, anxious knot.

"Yep. Holidays. Birthdays. Pretty much anytime anyone has a big deal going on, you'll have to be there. It's required."

"That sounds like a pain." She spoke softly, but her lips curved into a trembling smile.

"Yeah, I'm getting pretty good at this dad stuff.

So, you know, if you need advice or anything…" He laughed. "I'm just kidding. But seriously, go take a nap, young lady. You were driving all night and if you insist on going back tonight, you need some sleep."

She rolled her eyes, but as she turned away, she was smiling.

Garrett swayed back and forth with Charlotte. His mom used to say they were a family who believed in do-overs—because God gave them the biggest do-over. It was called grace.

Brooklyn needed a do-over. He could give her one by sharing his family with her. This, at least, made sense.

His feelings for Abby…less sense. That uneasy feeling settled in the pit of his stomach. This experience with Charlotte had shown him that he wasn't cut out to be worried all the time.

Abby's work was risky—obviously—she'd been shot on assignment. There was always going to be a need for her somewhere in the world. And just like she did last week, she would go.

Could he really get used to watching her walk out the door not knowing if or when she'd come back to him?

He pressed his thumb and finger against his eyes at the bridge of his nose, but tears welled up anyway. He loved her. He just wasn't sure he could deal with the threat of losing her.

When this was all over and Charlotte was out of the woods, he and Abby needed to have a long, serious talk. They'd grown so close. He couldn't deny his feelings for her.

But he had to lay his doubts on the table if they had any possibility of a future. And he wasn't looking forward to it.

* * *

It was five long days and nights before Charlotte was fever-free and discharged, but finally, Garrett was on his way back to the cabin with Charlotte. Abby slid a chicken casserole into the oven. She'd come over with some groceries and the idea of cooking dinner so Garrett wouldn't have to stop with Charlotte on the way home.

Winter's last gasp had dropped the temperature into the fifties and rather than turn the heat on, she'd started a fire in the fireplace. With the place tidied, candles lit and Elvis asleep on the rag rug in front of the hearth, the small cabin felt cozy and homey.

Elvis lifted his head and woofed softly. Abby heard Garrett's SUV pull up in front. She checked the room one last time for anything out of place before she opened the door, skipping down the porch steps and grabbing his bag while he released the infant car seat and brought Charlotte in.

"It smells so good in here. Looks good, too. I might cry." Garrett laughed as he unbuckled Charlotte and lifted her into his arms. "I know we were only gone five days but it felt like a month."

He kissed Charlotte on the head and put her in her favorite swing. She seemed happy to be there, taking her pacifier immediately, her eyelids already drooping.

"Charlotte looks so much better." Abby handed Garrett a glass of tea.

He dropped onto the couch, stretching his legs out. "I'm so glad to be home."

"Me, too." She choked on the words, with a laugh. "I mean, I'm glad you're home, too."

"You didn't even get a breather when you got back from California." He smiled at her. "You must be tired."

"I am, but actually, being away gave me some time to think about things."

He raised an eyebrow. "Like what?"

"It's strange—I've been going from disaster to disaster for so long that it took me a while to realize that real life isn't just about triage and stopping the bleeding."

She could feel his eyes on her, but he didn't say anything. Looking into the fire where the flames leaped and glowed, she slowed her thoughts, just focusing on the moment together.

For the first time in days, they had nowhere to be. Nothing to do. No crisis. The hum of the baby swing, the peacefulness of the sleeping baby, the crackle and pop from the fireplace. These were things she'd missed as she'd bounced from job to job.

But Garrett didn't seem to want to talk tonight.

"Maybe we should talk about this later," she backpedaled.

From somewhere he dragged up a smile. "No, I want to hear what you're thinking."

Abby scratched her head. "I'm not sure I'm making sense, but when I went to California, I realized that I really have lived my life from one catastrophe to the next. All crisis management, all the time. I loved my job—I do love it. But real life should have ebb and flow. Sometimes things happen and you can work *through* them. You taught me that. You, Nash's mom Melanie, Brooklyn. You inspire me to be brave, too."

"You're already brave, Abby." He looked down,

shifted away from her, glanced at his watch. "It's almost time for Charlotte's bottle. I need to get it ready."

In the kitchen, he pulled out a couple of bottles and a can of formula, before he braced his hands on the counter and let his head drop.

Wary now, Abby followed him. "What's going on? What aren't you telling me?"

"Nothing." He scowled. "It's just—you make a difference in people's lives. Go places other people wouldn't dream of going. You got *shot* and still went back to work. If that's not brave, what is?"

"Staying." She slid her hands down his arms and fitted them into his hands. "For me, staying is what takes courage. I've lived so long in black and white I forgot there was a whole world of color in between. I want the color, Garrett. Laughs and family dinners and picnics in the park."

His eyes met hers and held as he slowly brought his head up. "Abby—"

"I don't know how to belong yet—I never have before. But I'd really like to figure it out. With you." Her lips trembled and she pressed them together, holding her breath as she waited for him to say something.

A note of hope crept into his voice. "You're planning to quit your job?"

"Not completely, no. I'll still be traveling some."

Shaking his head, he took a step back, away from her, putting his hands up between them. "I can't do this, Abby. You keep your feelings all tucked away in neat little packages. I'm not like that."

The words were a slap. "I don't even know what that means."

"You're just...calm." He made a motion somewhere in the direction of her midsection. "I don't know how you do it."

She narrowed her eyes, anxiety and awkwardness gone, replaced by anger. "You think I don't have feelings just because I don't wrap my compassion around me like armor?"

"That's not what I said."

"Maybe I hold them close, but I have *feelings*, Garrett. Deep feelings. For example, I—"

Love you.

She swallowed the words because she knew he wouldn't accept them. He obviously wasn't ready to hear them and she sure didn't want to put them out there just to get them pushed aside. "Okay, then. I'm going to go."

"I'm sorry, Abby. I want to believe we could make this work, but I can't live a life where I'm always waiting for you to run away when things get hard. I can't do that to Charlotte."

Her heart felt like it was literally breaking. She'd put her hopes on the line with him and he'd stepped on them. Ground them into dust, not because he didn't care about her, but because he didn't care enough to risk getting hurt.

"You can use Charlotte as an excuse, and you might even buy into it, but I'm not the one running here. You are." Picking up her purse and keys from the end table, she turned back to face him. "Your casserole will be done in ten minutes."

He was standing in the middle of the kitchen, grief etched on his face, his hands held out as if in appeal.

"Abby, when you leave, you take my heart with you. I wouldn't survive if you didn't come back."

Abby shook her head. "I was wrong about you being brave. When you care about something, you fight for it. You don't give up because you're scared of what *might* happen. Come on, Elvis."

Abby walked out the door and closed it gently. She let Elvis into the backseat, got in her car and drove to the end of the driveway. Put it in Park, laid her head on the steering wheel and sobbed.

Elvis poked his head between the seats and licked her ear. She let out a strangled laugh, wrapping her arm around his neck. "I messed up, buddy."

Boy, did she. All those times she'd thought to herself that getting involved with Garrett was a bad idea? She should've listened to the voice of warning.

She picked up her phone and opened her text message app. Her thumb hovered over her boss's name. Surely there was a disaster somewhere in the world that could use her expertise.

Being in love was terrible. Maybe there was something essential missing from her because she didn't get it. If this was what being in love felt like, she wanted no part of it.

Chapter Seventeen

Three days after Abby walked out, Garrett scrubbed the feeding troughs in the barn with a stiff-bristled brush and hot soapy water. He'd gone through sadness and anger and was firmly in the self-delusion phase of grieving the loss of his relationship with Abby. It had hurt, no denying that. But he wasn't giving in to it. He'd done the right thing.

Any doubt he'd felt had been shoved down, patched and plastered over. He wasn't going to think about it.

While Garrett worked on the troughs, Devin was in one of the stalls, humming along to the country music station while he shoveled out the old straw, forking it into a wheelbarrow. Tanner worked behind them, making minor repairs. It would be a long day of mucking and maintenance, but it was a necessity on the farm if they wanted their animals to stay healthy.

Devin stopped singing. "Hey, Garrett, where's Abby? Lacey figured she'd be by to help with Charlotte today."

Garrett's hand paused midscrub at Devin's question. "Ah—she's not going to be coming around anymore."

Devin's head swiveled toward him. He leaned forward on the pitchfork. "What do you mean, she's not gonna be coming around here anymore?"

"I mean, we broke up. Except we weren't really together to start with so I don't even know if 'breaking up' is what you'd call it."

"Wow." Devin limped toward the bale of fresh hay and started sifting it onto the floor of the stall. "So after all that, she decided she wasn't going to stick around? That's kind of jerky."

Garrett paused again, a queasy feeling starting in his stomach. "That's not exactly what happened."

Tanner's voice came from the next stall over. "Look, I wasn't going to say anything because I figured it was none of my business. But she was sitting at the end of the driveway when I turned in the other night, crying her eyes out."

Now that was a piece of information Garrett didn't know. The patch job on his wall of denial was starting to crumble. He made a desperate gambit to shore it up. "She told me she'd decided to stay in Red Hill Springs, but she wasn't planning to quit her work in disaster areas."

"So?" Devin tossed the word over his shoulder as he moved to the back of the stall. "Tanner, there's a loose board in here."

"So, it's not a great way to build a relationship if one person is jetting off to disaster areas all the time. There's no way that was going to end good. Right?"

"I got it. You ended things with her so you wouldn't get hurt." Tanner calmly pounded the loose nail back into the wall with one hand and sanded down the splintered area around it with the other.

"Well, yeah. And Charlotte, too. I have someone else to think about besides myself right now." He rinsed out the trough with a bucket of clean water, watching it drain onto the dirt floor of the barn.

Devin shook his head. "Nope. I'm not buying it. You're making assumptions based on fear about what you think she's going to do. You don't know."

Garrett rolled his eyes. "We should've never let you go to therapy."

Tanner cleared his throat with a pointed look at Garrett, who squirmed under his older brother's scrutiny.

"Sorry," he muttered to Devin.

"No problem." Devin shrugged. "I know from personal experience how bad it stinks to be called out on something like this, but this is on you, bro. You broke her heart and you did it because you were scared."

His self-delusion buckling under the weight of Devin's words, Garrett stammered out an excuse. "I don't think—I mean, yeah, I was scared. But with good reason. It wasn't going to work out."

"What wasn't going to work out?" Lacey's voice came from the door.

"Garrett broke up with Abby." Devin's smile split his face as he tattled on Garrett to Lacey. He was actually enjoying this.

"What?" Lacey plopped a large orange water cooler onto a table by the door, along with a stack of disposable cups. "Tell me everything. Start at the beginning."

Garrett looked at the ceiling, praying for guidance. He hadn't expected so many questions, which—in retrospect, knowing his family—was a miscalculation on his part. He might as well go through the whole thing and maybe then they would let it go. "Okay, so the other night when I brought Charlotte home from the hospital, Abby was here. She made a casserole and had the house all cleaned up and stuff."

"Oh, yeah," Devin said. "She's a horrible person."

Garrett scowled at him. "Do you want to hear the whole story or not?"

"My bad. Continue." Devin limped past Garrett and picked up a rake.

"So Abby cooked dinner and she said…" Lacey prompted.

"She said she'd realized that traveling from one disaster area to the next, she'd never learned to work through things. She'd never stayed anywhere. Never belonged anywhere. She wanted to try to figure out how." He paused, the next words hard to say. "With me."

Lacey's eyes were glossy with tears. "She told you she wanted to stay in Red Hill Springs?"

"Yeah." He put his brush down on the edge of the trough, beginning to realize he'd made a terrible mistake. Abby was amazing. She'd been here every step of the way for him with Charlotte. She understood him in a way no one else really did.

He didn't know why he was so confused. "But I asked her if she was going to keep doing disaster work and she said yes. After all we've been through as a family, I just can't risk…"

His voice trailed off. He shook his head.

Tanner's eyes were steady on his. "Can't risk loving her?"

Garrett nodded, the ache in his throat too large to speak around.

Devin dropped the hose and walked over, gripping Garrett's shoulder in one strong hand. "I hate to break it to you, but I think it's too late for that. I think you already do."

"I sent her away." His voice was a hoarse whisper.

Tanner nodded. "You did. And you have to own that, but it's not over. If you love her, don't let her get away without a fight."

"I have to go." He turned to Lacey. "Can you—"

"I'll watch Charlotte. You go fix this."

Garrett left the barn at a run. He had to find her.

He'd made a terrible mistake.

What if he was already too late?

Garrett took the turn into Abby's driveway fast, his heart racing at a painful clip. The words *too late, too late, too late* were circling in an endless loop in his head.

He pulled up at the house, barreled out of the car and up the stairs to the front door. His feet stumbled to a stop as he saw a haphazard pile of baby things by the front door. Charlotte's bouncy seat and portable crib Abby had bought. A tote bag full of diapers and bibs and tiny pink clothes that tore at his heart.

The door was cracked and he pushed it open. He didn't even have to call out her name. The house was empty. All of the peace and light that Abby had brought was gone. The rental was spotless, not a speck of dust anywhere, and not a sign of life.

His shoulders dropped. He really had lost her. She

was somewhere in the world, making a difference in the lives of children, but he had no way of knowing where.

"Garrett?" Jules Quinn walked in through the door with an armload of fluffy white towels. "If you're looking for Abby, she's already gone. I'm getting the place ready for new renters. They're coming in tomorrow."

"I figured." He looked around the living room, memories flooding over him of the time he'd spent here with Abby, learning how to be a dad, laughing and healing. Falling in love.

He'd really made a mess of things. His feelings had been so intense from the beginning with Abby, which he guessed should've been his first sign that things were different with her. No one else had even come close.

With a sigh, he started for the door.

"You might be able to find her at her new place."

He slowly turned back. "New place?"

Jules smiled. "She signed a lease on that little house on the river bluff, next door to Jordan and Ash."

Relief nearly buckled his knees. "She's staying."

With a laugh, Jules nudged him out the door. "I think you need to talk to her about that."

"I'm going right now. I thought I'd lost her. I'm not going to make that mistake again."

Abby toed open the old screen door that led to her new front porch. There was an ancient metal glider in desperate need of a paint job and a view of the river that was worth a lot more than she was paying in rent. She took in a deep breath and let it slowly out.

Garrett's rejection had crushed her, but she wasn't going to let that stop her. She'd found a home and a community in Red Hill Springs. For the first time, she could see past the awkward and past the hard. She could have roots here. People who cared about her, if she would let them in. And she was determined not to hide behind her calling anymore.

Elvis was happy to roll in the grass in the sunshine or chase the nasty tennis ball he'd unearthed from one of the flower beds. And until she could put her feelings for Garrett to rest, there were plenty of projects to be done. Projects that she could pour her blood, sweat and tears into.

Like the sunshine soaking into her skin, the babble of the river as it skimmed across the rocks was soothing. Peaceful. It may not be the life in Red Hill Springs that she'd imagined, but it was going to be good.

Behind her, she heard a car coming up the dirt road that led through the woods and to her house. Wynn had said she was stopping by this afternoon with a housewarming present, so when the car door slammed shut, Abby turned, mustering up her best smile.

Garrett stood there, leaning casually against his car in a position reminiscent of the day she'd left for California. She froze, her smile fading.

She wasn't ready to see him. She wasn't sure she could hold it together with him and she desperately wanted to hold it together.

He was wearing jeans and boots and a faded law school T-shirt. He looked good, relaxed, which for some reason made her angry. Her chest ached with the effort of not reacting. Elvis dropped the tennis ball and trotted over to stand beside her.

"Jules told me where I could find you. I hope it's

okay that I came." He shoved his hands into his pockets. She could see the tension in his muscular arms and shoulders which made her feel marginally better.

"*Why* did you come, Garrett?"

He walked closer to her, his eyes on the grass, his long dark eyelashes a smudge against his tan skin. She hated that she noticed that. She wanted to hate him. No, that wasn't right. She didn't want to hate him. She wanted to feel nothing.

But she didn't. She hurt in a million places that she didn't even know she could hurt. In a way, though, maybe she should thank him. He'd broken her heart, but he'd also shown her that she was stronger than she knew. She was brave—brave enough to stay and she didn't need him to be the reason. It was enough that she wanted her roots to be here.

He stopped in front of her, hands still in his pockets. "I owe you an apology."

"Okay."

"I can't even say 'in my defense,' because I don't have a defense. I just messed up." He paused, his eyebrows drawing together. "When Charlotte got sick, all I could think about was how I couldn't protect her. And when Brooklyn came, it just made that feeling worse. I've gone all these years thinking that I'd come through my parents' deaths without any lasting scars. I was wrong."

She rubbed the spot between her eyes with her fingers and then dropped her hand. "I'm not sure what this has to do with me."

He squinted against the bright sun glinting off the water. "When my parents died, I lost my center, my safety. And I pushed down my feelings so much that I believed my own lies to myself, that I'd overcome it."

He was confirming what she'd instinctively understood about him—that he'd tried to control life in the only way he could. And in that regard, he wasn't so different from her. "You thought if somehow you could weight the scales toward the good, it would mitigate the bad?"

When he nodded, she said, "But life doesn't work that way. I can vouch for that."

"Yeah. I've kind of figured that out." He shook his head. "I love my brothers, don't get me wrong, but Charlotte… I've never felt love like that. She stole my heart without even trying and I let her, knowing I would never get it back, not in one piece."

Abby's eyes stung and she blinked back the tears. She would not shed them. Not in front of him.

Garrett let out a short mirthless laugh. "And then I met you. Before I could stop myself, I was falling for you. It was like realizing this solid rock I thought I'd been on all these years was really quicksand and I didn't even know it until I was halfway under."

Abby took a step back, away from him. She didn't want an explanation for why he couldn't be with her, not when she knew that at the end of it, he would still walk away. "Garrett, you don't have to do this. It's fine. I'm fine."

"I do have to do this, though. Because the other night, when you said you wanted to stay in Red Hill Springs, that you wanted to figure it out with me… coming right on the heels of almost losing Charlotte, I couldn't see past how literally terrified I was."

She took a deep breath. "Did you know when I was a little girl, I always had a bag packed?"

"I didn't know that."

"I kept it under my bed in case I had to leave. My aunt wasn't unkind, she just didn't know how to deal with me, so I kept the bag ready and I learned not to count on anyone else. But that kind of independence comes at a cost."

Rubbing dampness away from his eyes with his thumb, Garrett voice was hoarse with emotion as he said, "Someone should've been there for you."

He was right. Someone should've been, but that wasn't her point. "I've unpacked my bag, Garrett. I'm staying in Red Hill Springs. I hope I don't cause you pain by being here, but I'm not leaving. Not this time."

Garrett held out his hands for hers, but she couldn't make herself reach for them.

He held them out anyway. "Abby, you are the most amazing, beautiful, perfect woman and when I said I wouldn't survive it if you didn't come back, I meant it. That night, I wasn't sure I could trust your feelings."

Her heart, which she thought had been broken, shattered into jagged pieces. She took another step back, resisting the urge to run into the house and slam the door and lock it. Once again, someone she cared about was looking at her and deciding she wasn't worth the trouble.

"I'm messing this up." He stabbed his fingers into his hair and the simple gesture reminded her: this was Garrett, the man who'd bought a ten-thousand-dollar stroller for a mom who couldn't afford it. The same man who'd found a baby on his doorstep and become a parent—a good one—in an instant. The same man who'd left chicken potpie on her doorstep when she'd been exhausted after a long day at work.

She stared at his hands—strong, work worn, open—then slowly slid hers into them.

He tightened his grip and swallowed hard. "That night, I didn't know if I could trust your feelings, but then I realized—I can trust mine. I love you. I love you so much that my heart is never going to be the same. And whether you're here or California or Timbuktu, that's not going to change."

The tears she'd refused to shed spilled down her face. "I love you, too."

"I know." His voice was full of wonder as he tugged her forward into his arms and his lips hovered over hers. "Just like I know I don't deserve you, but I promise, when you go away, I'll be right here waiting for you to come home."

He was so tantalizingly close, but she didn't make him close the distance. She brushed her lips across his, laughing against his mouth when he kissed her back.

Finally. *Finally.*

He lifted his head and tenderly touched his forehead to hers as he let out a long, slow breath of relief. "Oh, I almost forgot. I brought you something—a housewarming gift, you could say."

He went back to the car and reached through the open window, pulling out a kitten, cupping it in his hands. "She's still a little small, but she's feisty."

"Oh, Garrett, I love her." She reached for the calico kitten, who crawled up her shirt, purring as she dug in with her tiny claws. Abby laughed and put her down on the ground, where she stalked Elvis, her little tail sword straight. "Be nice, Frances."

Garrett looked down at her, his heart in his eyes. "I'm not a prize. I'm a little broken, a little bit cracked, but you—you light up all the dark places, for me and for Charlotte. And I want to spend the rest of my life making you as happy as you make us every day. Please marry me?"

"Yes!" Abby laughed and tilted her face up, pressing her lips against his as his arms closed around her, lifting her off her feet. "Yes. Yes. Yes."

She slid to the ground, wrapped her arms around him and tucked her head into the crook of his neck, where it fit perfectly.

And she realized that in this spot—right here in Garrett's arms—she'd found the place where she belonged.

Epilogue

Devin and Tanner stood to Garrett's left. Wynn and Lacey stood to Abby's right. The whole place smelled like flowers, which seemed somehow wrong to Garrett. Courtrooms were supposed to smell like old leather and wood polish.

Abby squeezed his hand and he looked down at her. She was dressed simply in a lace dress, a flower crown in her hair. And she was beautiful—her love for him, along with her healthy sense of humor, shining in her eyes.

At the judge's direction, Abby slid the heavy gold band onto the fourth finger of his left hand. "Garrett, I give you this ring as a sign of our constant faith and abiding love. With this ring, I thee wed."

And then it was his turn.

He took his mother's ring from Devin and slid it onto Abby's finger. His voice shook with emotion as he said, "I give you this ring as a sign of my solemn vow. With all that I have and all that I am, I will honor you. With this ring, I thee wed."

Wynn was openly sniffling as the judge said, "By the power vested in me by the state of Alabama, I now declare you husband and wife. Garrett, you may kiss your bride."

Abby wasn't having any of that. She threw her arms around his neck and planted one on him. Wynn let out a whoop. The many people who filled the courtroom and spilled out into the hall clapped and cheered.

The judge rounded the bench and picked up her gavel, tapping it to get everyone's attention. "And now, we have one more very important matter to attend to. Abby and Garrett, please raise your right hands and repeat after me. I will tell the truth, the whole truth and nothing but the truth, so help me, God."

Garrett had heard those words hundreds of times, had said them nearly as many, before testifying as a guardian ad litem. But saying them today, on the most important day of his life, was different.

Weightier. He reached for his baby girl. Charlotte was starting to sit up now and when he settled her on his arm, she grabbed his face and squealed.

The judge laughed. "Abby and Garrett, will you provide a loving, lifelong home for Charlotte?"

Together, they answered. "Yes, we will."

"Will you confer upon her the same rights and benefits as you would a biological child, should you have one?"

Again, they answered yes.

"What name are you giving this child?"

Garrett looked down into Abby's eyes and back at the judge, with a smile. "Charlotte Abigail Cole."

Without warning, Charlotte dove forward into Abby's

arms. Abby snuggled her close, eliciting a sigh from their audience as Charlotte laid her head on Abby's shoulder. Garrett put his arm around both of them and wondered for the millionth time how he could've possibly gotten so lucky.

"I don't have to ask Charlotte what she thinks about this situation. That's pretty obvious." The judge grinned down at them.

Garrett glanced back to the first row, where Brooklyn was sitting with Elvis. Her eyes were shiny, but she nodded. She was part of their family, too.

With a flourish, the judge signed the adoption decree on the desk in front of her. "I'm so honored to have been a part of the creation of a brand new family today. Congratulations to the newlyweds *and* to the newest member of the Cole family. I wish you all a very happy future together."

Later that night, after all the cake had been eaten and their friends had gone home, Abby brought the baby monitor out onto the porch where Garrett was waiting for her. They were planning to go on a honeymoon, but wanted to be with Charlotte tonight, on their very first night as a family.

Abby took Garrett's hand and drew him out into moonlight. It was a warm summer night, a multitude of stars brilliant against the black sky. Fireflies twinkled around them, winking off, only to reappear a few feet away. And the rustling of the river in the background was the only music they needed.

"It was a perfect day, Mrs. Cole. A dream come true." Garrett held out his arms and she stepped into them.

Swaying back and forth, she giggled as he whirled her around, bare feet spinning in the grass. When she was upright again, he wrapped his arms around her waist, pulling her close. "I never even dreamed anything like this would happen for me. I love you, Garrett."

"I love you, too." He pressed a kiss to her hair and rested his chin on her head with a contented sigh.

And, as she stood in his arms, with their baby sleeping safely inside, she could only think how blessed she was that out of all the places on the planet, she chose this one.

God had brought their family together here.

Right where they all belonged.

* * * * *

If you loved this story, check out
The Cowboy's Twin Surprise
*from author Stephanie Dees,
the first book in the
Triple Creek Cowboys series!*

*And be sure to pick up the books
from her previous series,
Family Blessings*

The Dad Next Door
A Baby for the Doctor
Their Secret Baby Bond
The Marriage Bargain

Available now from Love Inspired!
Find more great reads at www.LoveInspired.com

Dear Reader,

Some characters are special. I knew from the first time Garrett appeared in a scene with his unruly hair and ready smile that he was one of those. He needed a heroine who could see through his abundant charm to his generous heart.

Abby's just that kind of heroine. Despite all she's been through in her life, she has a quiet joy that spills over to everyone around her and a firm strength that is undeniable.

Each of them has to let go of their fear (and their white-knuckle grip on control) before they can step together into the future God has waiting for them, but oh, is it worth the risk!

You're in my prayers always, my friends, and I love hearing from you! You can contact me via my website, www.stephaniedees.com, on Facebook at www.facebook.com/authorstephaniedees, and on Instagram at www.instagram.com/authorstephaniedees.

Warmly,
Stephanie

COMING NEXT MONTH FROM
Love Inspired

Available March 17, 2020

AN AMISH EASTER WISH
Green Mountain Blessings • by Jo Ann Brown

Overseeing kitchen volunteers while the community rebuilds after a flood, Abby Kauffman doesn't expect to get in between *Englischer* David Riehl and the orphaned teenager he's raising. Now she's determined to bring them closer together...but could Abby be the missing ingredient to this makeshift family?

THE AMISH NURSE'S SUITOR
Amish of Serenity Ridge • by Carrie Lighte

Rachel Blank's dream of becoming a nurse took her into the *Englisch* world, but now her sick brother needs her help. She'll handle the administrative side of his business, but only temporarily—especially since she doesn't get along with his partner, Arden Esh. But will falling in love change her plans?

THE COWBOY'S SECRET
Wyoming Sweethearts • by Jill Kemerer

When Dylan Kingsley arrives in town to meet his niece, the baby's guardian, Gabby Stover, doesn't quite trust the man she assumes is a drifter. He can spend time with little Phoebe only if he follows Gabby's rules—starting with getting a job. But she never imagines he's secretly a millionaire...

HOPING FOR A FATHER
The Calhoun Cowboys • by Lois Richer

Returning home to help run the family ranch when his parents are injured, Drew Calhoun knows he'll have to work with his ex—but doesn't know that he's a father. Mandy Brown kept his daughter a secret, but now that the truth's out, is he ready to be a dad?

LEARNING TO TRUST
Golden Grove • by Ruth Logan Herne

While widower Tug Moyer isn't looking for a new wife, his eight-year-old daughter is convinced he needs one—and that her social media plea will bring his perfect match. The response is high, but nobody seems quite right...except her teacher, Christa Alero, who insists she isn't interested.

HILL COUNTRY REDEMPTION
Hill Country Cowboys • by Shannon Taylor Vannatter

Larae Collins is determined to build her childhood ranch into a rodeo, but she needs animals—and her ex-boyfriend who lives next door is the local provider. Larae's not sure Rance Shepherd plans to stick around...so telling him he has a daughter is out of the question. But can she really keep that secret?

The soup scalded Arden's tongue and gave him something to distract himself from the topsy-turvy way he was feeling. As he chugged down half a glass of milk, Rachel remarked how tired Ivan still seemed.

"*Jah*, he practically dozed off midsentence in his room."

"I'll have to wake him soon for his medication. And to check for a fever. They said to watch for that. A relapse of pneumonia can be even worse than the initial bout."

"You're going to need endurance, too."

"What?"

"You prayed I'd have endurance. You're going to need it, too," Arden explained. "There were a lot of nurses in the hospital, but here you're on your own."

"Don't you think I'm qualified to take care of him by myself?"

That wasn't what he'd meant at all. Arden was surprised by the plea for reassurance in Rachel's question. Usually, she seemed so confident. "I can't think of anyone better qualified to take care of him. But he's got a long road to recovery ahead, and you're going to need help so you don't wear yourself out."

"I told Hadassah I'd *wilkom* her help, but I don't think I can count on her. Joyce and Albert won't return from Canada for a couple more weeks, according to Ivan."

"In addition to Grace, there are others in the community who will be *hallich* to help."

"I don't know about that. I'm worried they'll stay away because of my presence. Maybe Ivan would have been better off without me here. Maybe my coming here was a mistake."

"*Neh.* It wasn't a mistake." Upon seeing the fragile vulnerability in Rachel's eyes, Arden's heart ballooned with compassion. "Trust me, the community will *kumme* to help."

"In that case, I'd better keep dessert and tea on hand," Rachel said, smiling once again.

"Does that mean we can't have a slice of that pie over there?"

"Of course it doesn't. And since Ivan has no appetite, you and I might as well have large pieces."

Supping with Rachel after a hard day's work, encouraging her and discussing Ivan's care as if he were…not a child, but *like* a child, felt… Well, it felt like how Arden always imagined it would feel if he had a family of his own. Which was probably why, half an hour later as he directed his horse toward home, Arden's stomach was full, but he couldn't shake the aching emptiness he felt inside.

She is going back, so I'd better not get too accustomed to her company, as pleasant as it's turning out to be.

Don't miss
The Amish Nurse's Suitor *by Carrie Lighte,*
available April 2020 wherever
Love Inspired books and ebooks are sold.

LoveInspired.com

LOVE INSPIRED

INSPIRATIONAL ROMANCE

UPLIFTING STORIES OF FAITH, FORGIVENESS AND HOPE.

Join our social communities to connect with other readers who share your love!

Sign up for the Love Inspired newsletter at **LoveInspired.com** to be the first to find out about upcoming titles, special promotions and exclusive content.

HARLEQUIN

Heartfelt or suspenseful, inspiring or passionate, Harlequin has your happily-ever-after.

With new books published every month, you are sure to find the satisfying escape you know you deserve.

HNEWS2020